Gravity

Kathleen Ryder

I0601066

DEDICATION

For anyone who has ever had an
unrequited crush, I feel your pain.

PROLOGUE - CASSIDY

"Why don't you ask Jax if he has any space free next year? Maybe he can teach Riley how to play the guitar?" Cassidy shrugged as she made the suggestion to her friend, Anna.

"I thought about that, but he's moving to Brisbane after Christmas," Anna sipped at her mug of hot tea, completely oblivious to what she had just done.

"What?! He is not," Cassidy scoffed, her heart pounding.

"Yeah, he is," Anna nodded nonchalantly, "Sarah found out at band practice today."

"You're kidding? Wow, usually they mention staff departures in the staff meetings, Jax certainly kept that quiet," Cassidy was surprised that her voice was still able to sound normal.

"Hmm, I guess so," Anna shrugged, helping herself to another biscuit.

"Did Sarah say why he was moving to Brisbane?" Cassidy couldn't resist asking.

"Apparently he's taken a job down there, just having a change, chasing new opportunities," Anna relayed.

"Goodness, I really can't believe it!" Cassidy exclaimed, hoping her true feelings didn't start showing through.

"I know, right?" Anna agreed. "He's been Sarah's music teacher for years. For so long, it started to feel like he was a part of the landscape here in Alice Springs. Naturally, she's really upset, we're not sure who will be taking over music next year, or even if it will still be offered. The other music teacher, Steve, is leaving too, his fiancé is over in India and so he will be going to be with her."

"Oh well, no loss there, he was weird."

"Wasn't he ever! Plus, he drove like a maniac, so obviously not a good role model for our kids."

"Surprising, though, he didn't even last a full twelve months. I guess desert living isn't for everyone."

"No, well, I always thought he was a bit of a delicate flower," Anna scrunched up her face with displeasure.

"I wonder if that is really why Jax is moving to Brisbane, or if there is another reason?" Cassidy mused.

"I think there is another reason," Anna leant forward, "I think he must be moving for love."

"Love?" Cassidy's eyebrows rose, she wasn't so convinced.

"Don't sound so sceptical," Anna laughed, "people do fall in love and make decisions based on that all the time."

"I know that, but Jax?"

"Look at the evidence," Anna continued, "I never ever see him at the shops, do you?"

"No," Cassidy had to admit that in all the time she had lived in Alice Springs, she had never once seen Jax at the supermarket.

"So, there you go, obviously someone must shop for him."

"Or maybe he eats out?" Cassidy knew how lame that sounded, no one ate out every night, but she couldn't help clutching at straws.

"Okay then, point number two," Anna held up two fingers, "Jax is always happy."

"Happiness is not a crime," Cassidy smiled indulgently at her friend.

"True, but in my experience, men are only happy if they are in a relationship."

"What? That's not true."

"Okay, maybe not," Anna conceded, "but Sarah said she saw him driving around with a woman, laughing at something together. She said they looked like a couple."

"Well, whatever the reason, it will be weird not seeing him around town anymore. Now, tell me about Sean, how is he liking his new job?" Cassidy changed the subject, not sure how much more talk of Jax she could handle. It wasn't her friend's fault that Cassidy was shocked by the news, she had no idea of Cassidy's past with Jax, no one did, Cassidy kept it quiet, secreted away deep in her soul where no one could touch it or mock it or ruin it as they did with everything else. Cassidy had kept it sacred, protected, no one knew how she felt, no one would ever know, she would never tell them.

Cassidy had had enough of people mocking her in her lifetime. There was no way she would give anyone the ammunition they needed to do it again. Instead, she kept her mouth shut, she rarely let her emotions show, and she dressed in an impenetrable armour designed to keep her safe. The side effect, of course, was that people thought that she didn't care, or wasn't interested, which couldn't have been further from the truth. For the very few people who saw past her appearance to the fiercely beautiful soul inside, she gave them her unwavering loyalty. She bathed them in a dazzling light of trust and love, she raised them up and cheered them on, allowing them into her inner circle, the cherished few who were called friends. Not many people made it, very few ever saw past her outer shell, those that did gained a friend for life. Cassidy knew who she was, and she knew how people saw her. She was happy in her skin and loved the curves that others hated, she was prone to saying the wrong thing; she spoke her mind and wasn't afraid to call people out for rude or unacceptable behaviour. She was fiercely protective of those she loved, and champion of the underdog. She had a loud and infectious laugh, and she made no apologies for who she was.

Cassidy knew that she wasn't for everyone, and she was okay with that. She had finally reached a place where she was comfortable in her own skin, and she was content with that. Mostly. Cassidy had days when she was lonely and wished that she had someone special in her life, but she had reached a point now where she didn't think that would ever happen. She knew that on some level, she was too damaged to expect a fairy-tale ending, years of neglect and abuse at the hands of her parents had shown her that her value and worth were negligible at best. She hid her scars well, but they were still there, festering away underneath her skin, oozing poison when she least expected it. She knew they would weep tonight, as would she. She would weep for all that she had lost, even though it had never been hers to start with. She would weep for lost opportunities, and unfulfilled dreams, for chances stolen from her, and a life unlived. Hours later, as Cassidy lay in bed in the dark, her fist stuffed in her mouth to avoid making a sound, the tears coursed down her cheeks. Jax was leaving Alice Springs. That was it, he was going. She was never going to see him again, she was losing everything that she had ever wanted, and no one even knew.

When the tears finally subsided, Cassidy fell into a restless sleep, waking as the first fingers of dawn began to creep across the sky, resignation stooping her shoulders. The house was silent, as it always was when she rose, the only other occupant, her faithful dog, Bella, fast asleep. As Cassidy made her first cup of coffee for the day, she briefly considered what would happen if she simply told Jax that she was going to miss him. She didn't think that he would be the kind of person to belittle her or mock her for admitting her feelings, she was just so used to being rejected that she didn't know where to start. It would make no difference, she knew that, and yet she wanted him to know that she would miss him, that someone would miss him and wish him well. Pulling out a sheet of paper from her desk drawer, Cassidy sat down and started to write, pouring her heart out onto the paper in front of her, hoping that somehow Jax would see through the words to the weight of emotion behind them, that he would know what she was trying to say to him.

Dear Jax,

I know that to you I am nothing more than the woman who helps out in the front office, but to me, you are so much more. I am devastated that you are moving to Brisbane, I know that might come as a surprise to you, but there you go. Don't get me wrong, I am so happy for you, you deserve every opportunity that comes your way, but I am going to miss you so very much. You see, to me, you are liquid sunshine. You have this warmth that just radiates from you and wraps everyone up. You are kind to everyone, even when others aren't. You always have time to stop and talk to people, and more than that, you listen, actually listen to others, as if they are the most important conversation you are having that day.

I have had a crush on you since the first day we met, do you remember that? I was working at the social security office, and you had come in to let us know you had a new job. I was struck by your looks, who wouldn't be, as well as by your words. There was just something about you, something intangible that spoke to my soul, something that sparked a fire within me. I couldn't tell you why, but at that moment I just knew that you were meant to be in my life, that you were my soul mate, and yes, I know how odd that sounds. That was ten years ago now, and I have never told you. I couldn't tell you. I was just so scared of being rejected, of being laughed at, that I never took a chance, on you, on us. I never gave you a chance to prove me wrong. I'm sorry about that, more sorry than you'll ever know.

The fear of your reaction, coupled with the knowledge that people like you don't end up with people like me, stopped me from ever saying anything. I thought I would have forever with you. I genuinely thought that you would always be in my orbit in some way. I never imagined that you would move away, how crazy is that? Even now, I can't tell you. I literally can't even speak to you, every time I try, I just get so tongue-tied and end up sounding foolish. So instead, I am writing this, in the hopes that you will read it and understand just how very much you have meant to me, even if you didn't know it.

I have no idea what might have happened if I had ever had the courage to tell you that I like you, that I would like to get to know you better. Maybe we would have gone out, maybe we would have discovered a spark to set us on fire. Maybe we would have found we had nothing in common and parted ways. I'll never know, and that haunts me, the what if's. Maybe, if you read this, if you feel something, or are simply curious, you can let me know. You have my email address and my phone number, you can text me or call me or email me or send a carrier pigeon (but don't really, my dog would not like that very much). A text message from you would make my year. And if you don't feel anything for me, I wish you find happiness in Brisbane. Above everything else, if you are happy, that would be enough for me.

I will miss you more than I can say.

Cassidy.

Later that afternoon, when Cassidy was starting to get ready to head home from work, she took her letter and placed it in a sealed envelope, and added it to a wrapped box of chocolates. If anyone asked, she would tell them that it was a going-away gift. When Steve came into the office to sign in the bus load of music students he had just collected, Cassidy gave him the wrapped gift.

"Steve, can you pass this along to Jax, please? One of the parents dropped it off for him, something about a leaving town gift?" Cassidy feigned knowledge.

"Sure thing," Steve winked at her, and she tried not to let her displeasure show. He was supposed to be engaged or married for goodness sake, not flirting with single women. With the gift clutched in one hand and his guitar in the other, Steve dashed from the front office to the music room, leaving Cassidy to simply hope that Jax got her note and that he read it and didn't merely throw it away.

Despite telling herself that she wasn't going to think about Jax anymore, not for any reason, Cassidy found that he was all she could think about. She tried not to get her hopes up, she really did, but every time her phone beeped, she jumped up to grab it, convinced that it would be from Jax, showing some kind of indication that he likes her, but it never was. After a couple of weeks of bouncing around, her heart stopping with every text message, Cassidy is forced to admit what she already knew, that Jax is simply not interested in her. She tried not to let it bother her, she really did, but she couldn't help it, she had lost him, she had lost everything that she had ever wanted, and worst of all, he was never hers to begin with.

CHAPTER ONE - JAX

Jax fingered the mandarins gently, rolling one around in the palm of his hand, before placing them back on the shelf with a sigh. Not quite ripe. That was the one thing he really detested about Alice Springs, the severe lack of quality fruit and vegetables. If he was planning on staying longer he could try to grow his own, but then again, he had lived here for ten years and had never managed to get started. Just another regret to add to his ever-growing list. He wandered across to the kiwi fruit and added a couple to his shopping trolley, turning suddenly at the sound of a familiar laugh, looking around the aisles of the fruit and vegetable section until he finally placed it. Cassidy. The woman who had worked in the front office of the school where he had taught music, he hadn't thought about her in months, yet it was oddly comforting to find her here, his own dose of familiarity. He turned his shopping trolley in her direction and ambled over slowly, not wanting to seem too eager.

"Hi, stranger," he greeted her with a smile. Jax saw surprise and shock flash in her eyes, mingled with the embarrassed flush of her skin.

"Jax...hi," she squeaked, "you're back, wow, that's really great."

"Not permanently, just here for the Easter break."

"Oh. Well, that's nice," she finally graced him with a smile. "It was nice to see you again," as she started to edge her trolley away from him, Jax was struck with a sudden sense of regret, and his hand shot out to stop her trolley.

"Cassidy, wait, would you like to have coffee with me?"

"Coffee?" Her brows knitted together.

"Yes," he nodded.

"With you?" She clarified.

"Yes," he chuckled at her confusion, "with me."

"Oh. Um... okay, when?"

"I was thinking now if that suits you?"

"Of course, sorry Jax, your question threw me," Cassidy admitted shyly. "I'll just go pay for these few things and take them out to the car," she gestured to the items in her shopping

13

trolley, "I'll meet you out the front in a few minutes."

Jax watched her go before hurrying through the checkout himself and returning his items to his own vehicle, catching up with Cassidy in the car park and walking with her through to the only café inside the shopping centre that was currently open.

"Do you have any plans while you're here or just a general catch-up with your friends?" Cassidy asked as she stirred sugar into her coffee cup.

"A little bit of both actually," Jax answered, "I'm heading down to the Scorched Festival tomorrow, it was something that had been planned before I moved away, so I knew I wanted to come back for it. We'll be playing a set there, some new music and some old favourites."

"Jax! That's fantastic! Gosh, I'm so proud of you." She reached across the table to squeeze his forearm.

"Thank you. You could come, you know."

"To the festival?"

"Sure, why not?"

He wasn't sure what had prompted him to actually invite her to attend with him, he knew his bandmates would rib him about it later when they were alone, but it just seemed natural. He sensed that Cassidy was about to make an excuse, to blow him off, and he suddenly wanted her to come with him.

"It could be fun, catching up with you," Jax played his trump card. He knew he shouldn't have; he had read Cassidy's letter before he left for Brisbane, he knew that she had fancied him, had for many years apparently, and most likely still did. He knew he shouldn't encourage her, not when he had no intention of pursuing a relationship with her, yet he couldn't seem to stop himself.

"Jax, I'm not sure that sounds like a good idea, wouldn't you rather spend the weekend with friends?"

"We're friends," he grinned over at her, "aren't we?"

"Friends? Yes, I guess we are," Cassidy smiled.

"Well, there you go then, come on, it'll be fun, I promise," he waggled his eyebrows at her, earning a laugh.

"Okay, fine, you've convinced me, I'll come."

Scorched Festival was exactly as Jax expected it to be, even wilder than in previous years if that was possible, and he wondered if Cassidy would actually enjoy it or if it would be too much for her. She didn't really seem like the type of person who would enjoy a music festival, let alone one held in the middle of the Australian desert in freezing cold temperatures, but maybe she would surprise him? After they had left the coffee shop yesterday they had gone their separate ways, Jax to catch up with his bandmates, and to tell them that Cassidy would be joining them, news which raised more than a few questions. Nonetheless, when Jax pulled up to Cassidy's house he found that he was excited at the prospect of seeing her again. The Scorched Festival was held several hours drive outside of Alice Springs, the road trip down there uneventful, Jax and Cassidy spent the time talking about musical tastes, their favourite books, and world events. The Scorched Festival was already packed by the time Jax pulled into a parking spot and started unloading his gear. He was grateful that he had booked ahead and managed to secure a campervan for the night, there was no way he was looking forward to having to set up a tent. He gave Cassidy a quick tour of the property before heading on stage with his bandmates to start setting up their equipment.

"Hey, I saw you from over there, you're hot!" A man's voice broke out over the sound of Jax and his bandmates tuning their instruments, and he looked over to the edge of the stage where Cassidy stood, a man dressed in nothing but body paint currently talking to her.

"Oh!" Cassidy looked surprised, had no one ever told her how hot she was? "Um, thank you, I like your body paint," Jax watched as her eyes travelled down the man's chest and further still until her mouth gaped open in an O at the realisation that the man was, in fact, completely naked underneath his paint.

"Hey, thanks! I thought it was neat, I'm hoping it will glow in the dark, you know, it could be fun to take a ride on the Chris Express," Jax rolled his eyes at the man's words.

"The Chris Express huh? That's a rather unfortunate name, isn't it? As tempting as it is, I'm allergic to body paint."

"Oh. Well, maybe it will wear off?" Jax didn't know why, but the hopeful expression in the man's eyes annoyed him.

"Maybe," Cassidy nodded. Jax hoped she was only being nice.

Jax didn't have time to dwell on Cassidy's answer or his feelings towards the festival goer, before long it was time to change into his band tee and get out on stage. Jax and his band had been playing events in Central Australia for a decade now and had garnered quite the reputation for having a unique sound of angst and raw emotion, psychedelic riffs and searing lyrics. The crowd that came out to support them had been the same crowd that had supported them through the long months of concert postponements and cancellations brought about by the Covid pandemic, there was a real sense of celebration in the air tonight, the audience was ready to party, and party hard. Jax was on a high by the end of their set, every time he had looked across at Cassidy she had been there in the wings, watching them, supporting them, supporting him. It was a heady feeling and once the curtains had been shut and his guitar placed carefully back in its case, Jax strode over to Cassidy, cupping her face and lowering his mouth down to claim hers in a kiss that was electric.

His fingers tangled in her hair, and he angled her face, his tongue delving deeper inside, tasting every inch he could. At this moment she was his, his air, his reward, his all. He didn't know where he ended and she began, so lost in the kiss he was, only reluctantly breaking away from her when he heard the catcalls of his bandmates. He watched quietly as she walked away, the roundness of her bottom sashaying from side to side. He wondered what it would feel like to have her weight settled on top of him, to be buried inside of her softness.

"Jax," Kane slapped him on the back, "what are you doing? Cassidy? Seriously?"

"I'm not doing anything, we're hanging out, that's all," he defended.

"With Cassidy?" Kane sounded confused.

"Yes, with Cassidy." When Kane didn't answer, Jax continued. "What's wrong with Cassidy?"

"Come on, seriously? She's not your type, she's far too curvy. Come on, Jax, you could have anyone here tonight, and you choose her?"

"Are you serious right now? You're an arsehole, Kane," Jax sent his friend a final scathing look before heading off stage to catch up with Cassidy.

He found her in the campervan, making tea, the domestic image completely jarring against the images floating around in his head. She looked up as he entered the van, a soft blush staining her cheeks.

"Jax, I-"

"Shh," he placed a finger on her soft lips, watching the way her eyes dilated and grew round at the familiarity of the touch. "I fully intend to kiss you, Cassidy," and with that, Jax brought his mouth down to meet hers, their tongues clashing for dominance, their kiss frantic with lust and longing. It was Cassidy that broke the kiss, gasping for air, staring at Jax through large blue eyes, clouded with lust and confusion.

"Cassie," Jax's voice was ragged as he took Cassidy's hand and slid it down his torso until it was flush against his hardened length, the material straining against his twitching member. "Don't doubt how much I want you, how much I want this, but if you don't want the same thing, I'll go sleep in the car."

"It isn't that, Jax. I want you, of course, I want you, who wouldn't? I just didn't think you'd want this with me," Cassidy gestured to the space between them.

"You want me," Jax stated, "and I want you," he stepped closer to Cassidy, sliding his arm around her waist and using the palm of his hand pressed into the small of her back to bring her flush against his body, groaning as her hips involuntarily bucked against his erection. He brought his mouth down to meet hers, his tongue softly parting her lips, entering her mouth with confidence. Jax tangled his hands in her hair and pulled lightly, angling her face so that he could deepen the kiss, wanting to taste every inch of her, needing to claim her as his own.

"Cassidy, wait, are you sure you want this?" Jax tore himself away from her mouth to ask. He had to know that this was what she wanted too, not just because she was caught up in the moment, he had to hear her say it.

"I'm sure," Cassidy looked up at him with flushed cheeks and swollen lips, her eyes glassy with lust. Stripping off his shirt, Jax gathered the hem of Cassidy's dress in his hands and lifted it up, over her head, tossing it on the floor behind him. His eyes never left Cassidy's face as his hands travelled around to her back, unhooking her bra and letting it fall away, her breasts springing free.

"Gorgeous," Jax sighed before he claimed one of Cassidy's soft breasts in his mouth, flicking his tongue over the already engorged pebble, before nipping it with his teeth, earning a hiss of pleasure from Cassidy.

He broke away from her long enough to undo his belt, kicking his jeans and boxer shorts off of his ankles, Cassidy's mouth falling open at the sight of his erection jutting out proudly. With a chuckle, Jax knelt in front of Cassidy, hooking his fingers over the waistband of her panties and sliding them down slowly, kissing along her thighs as he went, savouring the taste of her, the sounds of her breath hitching, until her panties were off, leaving her completely naked to him.

"Gorgeous," Jax whispered as he began to kiss his way back up her thighs, stopping at her core, her scent wafting over him, surrounding him. He parted her thighs, lifting one leg up over his shoulder, wanting to be closer, needing to be closer to her centre. With a deep groan, his tongue darted out to taste her seam with a single lick, Cassidy's hips bucking violently beneath him at the unexpected pleasure.

Needing no further urging, Jax plunged his tongue deep inside her core and ran it back and forth along the inside length of her, drinking in her wetness, savouring her taste. He moaned into her, flicked his tongue over her nub and then drew back, straightening up. Moving his mouth higher, Jax found Cassidy's sensitive bud, drawing it into his mouth and suckling hard, his hands holding her hips in place. He slid a hand between them, dipping a finger into her silky folds, testing her wetness before adding another finger.

"Mm-hmm, you're so wet, Cass, so perfect," he added a third finger, increasing the speed of his thrusts, "absolutely dripping. Who gets you this wet, tell me?"

"J-Jax, you, just you, always you," she panted out between gasps, writhing against his hand, trying to get closer, whimpering with need.

"Always? Do you think about this Cass, when you're alone at night?" He bit down on her bundle of nerves, Cassidy's hips bucking against his face.

"Yes!" She hissed.

"Do you touch yourself, Cass? You do, don't you?"

"Yes, yes, please, Jax, I need..." her hands fluttered at her sides.

"Show me, I want to see you touch yourself, Cass," Jax ordered. Cassidy's hand slid down until her long fingers had swirled in her dark curls, and he watched, fascinated, as her fingers tweaked and circled her sensitive nub, pulling and pinching, her tempo increasing faster and faster until he knew that she was close to release. Jax pounded his fingers in and out of her dripping core, twisting them with each thrust, increasing his rhythm faster and faster to match the strokes of her own fingers, relishing the feel of her moving in sync with him, thrusting her hips to take his fingers deeper inside her centre, moaning and screaming out his name as she came undone, shudders echoing through her body.

Once Cassidy had come down from her high, Jax stood and led her to the bed, watching, mesmerised, as Cassidy laid back against the bed and let her legs fall open, never breaking eye contact, giving him a perfect view of her silky folds waiting for him, already covered in her juices, just waiting for him to claim. Jax wasted no time, retrieving a condom from his wallet and sheathing himself before manoeuvring to kneel between her legs, the head of his throbbing length butting against her sensitive nub, causing Cassidy to shout out. He gripped his throbbing length in his hand, using it as a guide to thrust his thick shaft deep into her softness, a deep sigh of satisfaction leaving his body as her walls stretched to accommodate his length with a delighted shout from Cassidy. His mouth bent to enclose her puckered nipple, suckling firmly before his teeth grazed over the hardened nub, biting down gently, causing Cassidy to cry out and arch her back, thrusting her breasts towards him. Jax moved his hand between their heated bodies, touching and teasing her bundle of nerves as he moved inside her. He relished the very feel of her, rocking back and forth into her with long, slow, firm, deep strokes until he felt her climax building again. Jax began to move faster, frantic with need, so close to his release, rocking Cassidy in rhythm, fuelled by her cries for him to go faster, harder, deeper. Exploding together, Cassidy's walls gripped Jax's shaft tightly as he emptied his need deep inside of her, filling her.

Once their breathing had returned to normal, Jax slid his member from deep inside of Cassidy and scooted to the side of the bed to dispose of the condom, noticing with a frown that it had ripped.

CHAPTER TWO - CASSIDY

Cassidy stretched her arms above her head, her blanket shifting, the cold air hitting her breasts causing her nipples to pucker. She ached in the most delicious of ways, the gentle throb between her legs reminding her of every single thrust of the night before. With a yawn she rolled over, burrowing down beneath the covers, eyes still shut tight, not yet ready to face the day or the reality of the night before. Cassidy felt Jax stirring beside her, his fingers trailing up and down her spine, and opened her eyes reluctantly, smiling up at him through her lashes, the memory of last night hovering in the air between them. They had spent the entire night savouring each other, discovering what the other enjoyed, and even now, Cassidy felt wetness pool between her thighs at the thought of Jax's hands on her skin, at the knowledge of just what his wicked tongue could do to her. As Jax's gaze raked over her body, lingering on her breasts, she felt as if her entire skin was on fire, aching to be touched, to have him cool the burning flames that threatened to consume her. Leaning closer, Jax claimed her mouth with a kiss that left her in no doubt as to his desire for her. He slid a hand down to her centre, groaning into her mouth when he discovered that she was already wet for him. Shifting position, he pushed her knees up, letting them fall to her sides. She was completely open for him, splayed out, leaving nothing hidden.

He grinned wickedly up at her before teasing her sensitive nub with his tongue, claiming it with his mouth and sucking gently, as she writhed beneath him. He moved down to her silky folds, sliding his tongue inside, teasing, tasting her juices. Pulling her knees over his shoulders, he continued to slide his tongue in and out, flicking her nub with his fingers, pinching, rolling it between his thumb and forefinger as she bucked her hips beneath him, her breathing growing shallow.

"Jax!" She pleaded, clutching at his hips, "please!"

"Please what? Tell me what you need honey." His breath sent a cool breeze over her core, increasing her sensitivity.

"I want you. Inside me. Now!" She panted. Jax smiled against her before pushing himself to a sitting position and reaching across to the bedside table for a condom, unwrapping it and slipping it on. After their first-time last night, he had confessed to Cassidy that the condom had ripped, both of them beyond relieved when she had told him that she was on the contraceptive pill, the last thing either wanted was unplanned consequences.

With Cassidy's legs still dangling over his shoulders, Jax rose to his knees, leaning over her and using her legs as support, as he drove his hardened length into her, before pulling out fully and driving in again and again. Cassidy arched her back and bucked her hips to meet his powerful thrusts, screaming in pleasure as he drove in harder and deeper, his thick member hitting her G spot.

"Jax, oh my god, Jax, yes, yes!" Cassidy held nothing back as he moved within her, caressing his ego with her mews and moans, urging him deeper with her words.

"Come for me Cass," Jax ordered. Pulling his length out fully, he gave one final thrust all the way into her core, her walls tightening around his stiffened member as he pushed her over the edge while she screamed out his name with wild abandon. With one final thrust he exploded inside her, gripping her hips for support until totally spent, he collapsed beside her. Cassidy remained like that, wrapped up in Jax's arms until the sun started to push through the curtains of the campervan, and the sounds of other concertgoers starting to pack up reached her ears. Only then did she move, reluctantly, away from the warmth of his embrace, to dress in silence as he watched her, a look of contemplation on his face.

Cassidy doesn't speak, she doesn't think there is any reason for words, she knows that what happened last night, and this morning was a one-time only deal, she knew it wouldn't be repeated, not least of all because Jax now lived in Brisbane. More importantly though, despite what had happened last night and this morning, Cassidy knew that Jax didn't want a relationship with her. She wasn't stupid, she knew that she wasn't his type, in fact, she was as far removed from his type as was possible to get. Still, she couldn't bring herself to regret it, how could she, when it was all that she had ever wanted? She had lusted after this man for years, longed for him to notice her, to simply smile at her or to wink at her or to show her any kind of attention at all, and now he had. She would be content with that, she had her taste of Jax, she would make do, she would file it away in her memory for those nights when she needed someone to distract her, something to make her smile again. It would be her little secret, her precious, sacred, secret that she hoarded just for herself. Once she had finished dressing, Cassidy moved across to the kitchen portion of the campervan and busied herself with making two mugs of steaming hot coffee, needing to keep her hands busy to avoid them traitorously touching Jax again.

While Jax dresses and starts drinking his coffee, Cassidy potters around the campervan, tidying up and remaking the bed. With the campervan keys returned to the venue owner, and Jax's car packed tight with his band equipment, Cassidy and Jax started back on the journey to Alice Springs. Cassidy hadn't missed the way Jax glowered at his drummer this morning when he and the vocalist had arrived to help pack the car, it was obvious that something had happened between them last night, and Cassidy had the very uncomfortable feeling that she was somehow to blame. As curious as she was, she decided not to mention it, if Jax wanted her to know, then Jax would tell her himself. Cassidy had been dreading the drive home, especially after this morning, she had worried that the drive would be one long, awkward, empty, silence, but instead, it was as if nothing had changed. Jax regaled her with stories of his early band days, and Cassidy tried very hard not to be too much of a fan girl, the last thing she wanted was to be considered a groupie. It was bad enough that Jax knew just how long she had lusted, unsuccessfully, after him. It was rather mortifying actually, the more Cassidy thought about it, the more horrified she became.

When Jax had run out of stories to share, they discussed an author that they discovered they both loved, one who wrote cosmic horror, emphasising the horror of the unknowable and incomprehensible, rather than gore and shock, whose work encapsulated forbidden and dangerous knowledge, madness, superstition, fate and inevitability, nonhuman influences on humanity, and the risks associated with scientific discoveries. They were topics that fascinated Cassidy, especially fate and inevitability, which she strongly believed in. She knew that she was in the minority, but Cassidy firmly believed in soul mates and fate, she knew that certain things were unexplainable any other way. Jax was proof of that, not that she would ever tell him of course, but she wasn't even meant to be working with the public the day she first met him. A co-worker had called in sick and Cassidy had been pulled from her usual duties in the back of the office and asked to replace them last minute. If her co-worker hadn't fallen ill, Cassidy would never have met Jax that day, and their paths wouldn't have crossed for years. Cassidy knew that it was fate, she liked to think that it was fate's way of giving her a glimpse of her future, if only she remained patient.

When Jax pulled up outside of Cassidy's house, she turned to face him, a soft smile on her face.

"Jax, thank you for taking me with you to the concert, I'll never forget it."

"Cass, the pleasure was mine, believe me." Jax leant over to kiss her softly goodbye on her cheek, lingering a little longer than necessary.

"When are you heading back to Brisbane?" Cassidy asked, delaying the inevitable a little longer.

"Once I stop and buy petrol, I need to be back there the day after tomorrow."

"The day after tomorrow?! Jax, please promise me you'll drive carefully." Cassidy was shocked, the Alice Springs to Brisbane route usually took at least thirty-five hours of non-stop drive time, once you factored in breaks, the journey was a minimum of a three-day trip, five days with a single driver.

"I promise. I'll even text you when I have reception, so you can check up on me if you like."

"You can text me anytime you like, Jax, you don't need a reason to do so," Cassidy tried not to let her voice sound too excited.

"Anytime, huh? Well, maybe I will." His smirk had Cassidy rolling her eyes, she wondered just what he was planning.

"Just so we are clear, I am not going to check up on you or stalk your social media posts to make sure you got home safely. If you want me to know, you can tell me yourself."

"Fair enough, I will, I'll text you once I get back to Brisbane."

"Thank you." Cassidy leant across and kissed Jax's cheek quickly before popping the door open and standing up, opening the back door, and pulling her overnight bag out. "Safe travels, Jax." She turned on her heel and walked through her front gate, closing it firmly behind her, not wanting to see Jax driving away from her, not wanting to have that as the last image of him in her head. She counted to ten slowly, before peering over her fence just in time to see Jax's car turning the corner. "Please stay safe, I miss you," she whispered into the emptiness.

As Cassidy slipped into bed that night, snuggled up in her retro band shirt, flipping through her subscription television channels trying to find something to hold her interest, her thoughts turned to Jax. She hoped he was okay, she was sure that he was, but still, visions of him wrapped around a tree along the deserted section of highway haunted her and her fingers itched to send him a text message. It wouldn't hurt, would it? It wouldn't look that desperate, if she checked in with him, after all, they were friends, right? She picked up her mobile phone and checked the time on the screen, she would give him another thirty minutes, and then she would send him a message. Content with her decision, she settled in to rewatch her favourite English medical drama, set over seventy years ago and featuring an ensemble cast of midwives and their patients. Cassidy became so engrossed in her show that when her phone beeped alerting her to a text message, she jumped a mile high, scaring her dog off from the bottom of her bed.

Her eyes scanned the screen of her mobile phone, a large smile gracing her face when she saw Jax's name on the display. She skimmed the message quickly, Jax had made it to the halfway point, he had only needed to stop for fuel twice. Relieved, Cassidy reread the message slowly, mouthing out each of the words, analysing them, looking for nuances, feeling the way they felt on her tongue. He had made it to Quilpie, and was planning on staying there the night, before getting another early start tomorrow. Cassidy texted back that she was glad he had stopped, and that she hoped he would sleep well. After looking at the screen for endless seconds, Cassidy finally added a small x to the end of her message, after all, friends did that, didn't they? As she did every night, Cassidy muted her phone and turned it over so that it didn't disrupt her already insomniac riddled sleep, and finished watching her show, basking in the bliss that surrounded her from getting a text message from Jax. She knew that she shouldn't get her hopes up, that this didn't change anything, but just for tonight, she was going to pretend that it did, that this meant that he would continue to text her while he was in Brisbane, that he might actually miss her.

CHAPTER THREE - JAX

The journey from Alice Springs to Brisbane was uneventful, and as he had promised, once he had arrived back in Brisbane, Jax sent Cassidy a text message to let her know that he was home safe. It felt good to be back in Brisbane, he had relished the chance to leave Alice Springs, to get away, to get a new focus, and new perspective, and this job had meant a wonderful new opportunity for him. It wasn't quite what he had been expecting, but then he had come to realise that nothing ever was in life, one way or another. Cassidy sent him a return text message, a short thank you followed by a little x at the end of the message. Did friends do that? He wasn't sure, he didn't have many female friends, actually, he didn't have any that weren't related to him, he found that they generally wanted more than he was willing to provide. While he was content to have friends with benefits, or casual relationships, anything beyond that wasn't something he was looking for. He didn't want the dream of a white picket fence, a brood of kids, a dog, responsibilities, commitment, and he sure as heck didn't want to be accountable or reliable on anyone else. Nor did he want to be that for anyone else, he didn't want to be responsible for another person's happiness, he knew what a jerk he could be, usually without even trying, and no matter how many times he tried to do the right thing, he usually stuffed up. No, he was happy to float through life experiencing only friends with benefits, or casual relationships. No one got hurt that way, Jax included.

By the middle of his first week back, Jax found himself longing to hear Cassidy's voice and put it down to loneliness, that must be it, what else could it be? By the end of the week, he knew he was going to call her. Talking to Cassidy, about mundane things, about life and books, was surprisingly refreshing for Jax, and he started to wonder if maybe he could give a relationship with Cassidy a try. The long-distance thing would be hard, he knew that, but surely not impossible. Despite still not being sure if he wanted a relationship with Cassidy or not, Jax continued to call her most nights, and as the weeks went by, he found himself talking to her more and more on the phone, slowly disclosing little snippets of himself to her, slowly discovering her secrets in return. One night, about midway through the term, Jax was lying in bed talking to Cassidy on the phone, when she casually mentioned that they should do something over the Christmas break. They. As in the two of them. Jax and Cassidy. Together. Panicked, Jax made an excuse to get off the phone. Jax knew it was unfair of him, he knew that he was to blame for this, that he was the reason Cassidy had misunderstood the situation, that Cassidy was merely acting as any other female would, but he couldn't help but feel panic. There was no them or us, and he knew the moment that she had said it, that he didn't want there to be.

He was a jerk. He had deliberately used Cassidy, both in Alice Springs, to keep his bed warm, for a bit of fun for the weekend, and then over the phone once he had returned to Brisbane, to counteract his loneliness, his boredom. Great, what a mess he had made. Now he would need to tell her, or maybe he wouldn't, maybe he would just stop calling her, eventually, she would get the message, wouldn't she? Jax felt like a heel, yet another reminder of why he was staying single. He didn't enjoy hurting others, although he knew there would be a few women around he would beg to disagree, but he had always tried to do the right thing, for himself and for others. Yet he always stuffed everything up. For the people around him, relationships came easily, Jax didn't know how they did it. His brother was happily married, his mother had remarried after his father passed away, and even all of his cousins were happily in committed relationships. It was just him, the last single person in his family. When it came to women, Jax was a screw-up. During the next couple of weeks, Jax deliberately did not call Cassidy, and when she rang him, he let the call go to voicemail. Eventually, she stopped calling, and instead of being happy, Jax felt lost.

He had been back teaching for nine weeks now, and Jax was more than ready for a break. Although he hadn't planned on returning anytime soon, as the June school holidays approached, he found himself agreeing to spend his three-week break in Alice Springs, rehearsing with his band and working on some new songs and material. He had thought, briefly, about letting Cassidy know that he would be back in town but decided against it.

What would be the point? He had already screwed up enough with her, and he knew that if he called her again, she would answer, and then he wouldn't hesitate to have her back in his bed, he was certain of it. As tempting as it was, to feel Cassidy wrapped around him again, to be buried deep inside her, he was coming to Alice Springs to work on his music, not to screw around. If he reignited their friendship or casual relationship or whatever it was that he and Cassidy had, Jax knew he would spend the next three weeks in bed with her, and as tempting as that was, Jax knew that he couldn't do that to her. Even he had a line that he didn't cross, and deliberately using someone who he knew felt more for him than he did for her, just to satisfy him sexually, would be crossing it.

So instead, he said nothing. He simply packed his car back up again, and drove back up to Alice Springs, quietly arriving in town without fanfare or awkward reunions. His bandmates said nothing about Cassidy when Jax arrived alone, for which he was grateful. They had been out of line with their comments during the Scorched Festival, and even though he knew how much of a jerk he had been himself, there was no way he would stand for that behaviour from them, not towards Cassidy, who had done nothing wrong.

CHAPTER FOUR - CASSIDY

Cassidy lay in the dark, staring up at the ceiling, ignoring the tears cascading down her cheeks. She didn't know what had happened, no, that wasn't true, she knew what had happened, she had been stupid, that's what had happened. She had stupidly allowed herself to think that Jax calling her from Brisbane had actually meant something, that his friending her on his social media channels showed that he did like her, that there was something there between them. She had been an idiot, a stupid, stupid, fool. She should never have allowed herself to get carried away, should never have hoped for more, for anything, with Jax. She knew from the start that men like Jax never ended up with women like her, and yet she had foolishly allowed herself to get swept away with the possibilities, and now she was paying the price. He didn't want to talk to her, he had made that abundantly clear by ignoring all of her calls and allowing them to go to voicemail. At first, Cassidy had naively assumed that Jax had simply been busy, but it wasn't long until she had to admit the truth, that he was avoiding her.

She wished she knew why. Had she done something wrong? After all, he had been the one who had started calling her, not the other way around, and now that she had gotten used to hearing his voice, had grown accustomed to speaking to him every day, she was suddenly cut off from him. She felt bereft, a gaping emptiness inside where his voice used to be. She couldn't even blame him, not really, she knew how she was. She knew that she was hard to be around, high maintenance, difficult, after all, she had been told this often enough by others. It was her flaw, Cassidy knew that. She had always wanted too much, she had always wanted to be included, even as a child. Cassidy used to watch longingly as her family would go out to dinner or to the movies, or on day trips to the beach, and she used to think that one day, one day that would be her, one day she would have friends who loved her and who enjoyed her company, and they would make their own memories. Only, it never happened. Instead, whenever Cassidy had made a friend, she had been only too happy to say yes to anything they had needed, she had wanted to be able to help, had been happy to help them, her friends.

She hadn't thought anything of it, not at first anyway. It wasn't until much later, when the damage to her self-esteem had already been done, that she realised that she had been used. While she had been happily baking cake masterpieces for her friend's birthday celebrations, or babysitting their children, they had been going out with their friends, not with her, not including her. Cassidy had been devastated the first time her friend had thanked her for watching her child so that she could go out with friends, it had been a wake-up call, and shortly after that Cassidy had cut off all contact with everyone she had known and moved interstate to start fresh. It had taken a while to make friends in Alice Springs, Cassidy wasn't a drinker and therefore didn't frequent the local pubs, which seemed to be the only hangout that adults visited locally. Eventually, though, she had met a couple of people who had slowly become her friends, but even now, nearly a decade later, Cassidy still struggled with a sense of never being quite good enough for them.

A feeling that Jax had only reinforced with his actions. Cassidy sighed and rolled over onto her side. She hated how emotional she was at times, how weepy. She wished that she could just be normal, instead of always getting too involved, too invested. The only person it ended up hurting was herself, yet she couldn't stop. She loved big, that was just who she was. She never wanted her friends to doubt how much she valued them, never wanted them to wonder if they were good enough, the way that she so often did. So, she took all of the love that she had never had the chance to give to anyone, all of the love that she had been denied as a child, and she poured it into showing others that they mattered. It had become somewhat of a life mission for her, making sure that no one she knew ever felt invisible or unwanted the way she often did. She scrubbed at her cheeks with her hands, she really needed to stop crying, to stop feeling. She was good at that, freezing her emotions, acting as if nothing bothered her. She could do it again, she could do it now, she would do it now, she resolved to herself as she inhaled a deep breath.

She was usually only ever overly emotional now when she had her period, maybe that was the problem? Cassidy picked up her mobile phone from her bedside table and unlocked it, navigating to the calendar app and counting backwards, sitting bolt upright before recounting slower, to no avail. The numbers weren't wrong, she had missed her period. It was four days late. In all of her life, Cassidy's period had never been late before, you could set your watch by it. It was okay, she wouldn't panic, there was probably a logical reason, it was probably stress or...Cassidy couldn't think of a single logical reason for her period to be late. Panic started to well up inside her and she squashed it back down again. She would not panic, she would not overreact, she would not play the what-if game, no, instead, she would go to sleep, and if things hadn't returned to normal tomorrow, she would go to the chemist and buy a pregnancy test.

When Cassidy woke the following morning, her period still had not arrived, and she knew that she would need to go to the chemist and buy herself a pregnancy test, if for no other reason than to put her mind at ease. She showered and dressed slowly, lingering over breakfast, trying to delay the inevitable. She slunk into the chemist, feeling like a criminal, convinced that everyone there knew why she was there and what she was doing, certain that everyone was watching her, judging her. She found the aisle she wanted easily enough, but the sheer array of tests was mind-boggling. She just wanted a test that said pregnant or not pregnant, how hard was that? There were digital tests and non-digital tests, twin packs or single packs, those claiming to be accurate after the first day of a missed period and those claiming to be accurate after the first week of a missed period. In the end, Cassidy grabbed a twin box that claimed to be accurate ninety-nine per cent of the time and headed to the checkout. Turning the corner, Cassidy collided with something solid, hissing as her breath was knocked out of her.

Glancing up to apologise, Cassidy's eyes met Jax's eyes, and her apology died on her tongue, her mouth hanging open.

"Oh my gosh, I'm so sorry, are you all right? He can be a bit of an oaf at times." Cassidy turned to look at the woman who was speaking, the woman who was obviously with Jax. She was achingly beautiful, skinny with a head of luscious brunette hair, she was dressed in the cutest mini skirt and top that Cassidy had ever seen. Cassidy couldn't help but glance down at her own outfit, frumpy track pants and a navy tunic paired with a grey puffer jacket. She groaned internally, she didn't even know how to dress properly, no wonder people thought she was weird. She closed her eyes briefly against the sting of rejection, before taking a fortifying breath and answering.

"No, it's fine, it was completely my fault, I should have been paying attention." Cassidy wondered if Jax caught her double meaning.

CHAPTER FIVE - JAX

She should have been paying attention? Interesting choice of words. Seeing Cassidy again was like a punch in the guts for Jax, he never imagined that he would run into her, he certainly hadn't planned to, and in the chemist of all places. He hadn't missed the look of shock on her face when she had realised that it was him that she had run into, and he braced himself for the scene he thought would surely follow. Instead, she had surprised him, she had been polite and detached, as if everything was perfectly fine, as if he hadn't been a jerk to her. Jax was...surprised. He had expected her to be angry, snarky even. From past experiences with women, if they felt in the least way slighted, they tended to overreact, to become screaming versions of themselves. Or maybe that was just the women who had dated Jax, he wasn't sure. Cassidy looked as if she wanted the floor to swallow her whole, to disappear, and he didn't blame her he rather wished the same thing would happen to him. Jax shuffled uneasily on his feet, acutely aware of the ridiculously large container of condoms he currently held in his hands. Great, now she was going to think he was some kind of addict, why had he let Carmen talk him into this? He should have said no, he should have made her go and buy them herself, regardless of her embarrassment.

He avoided Cassidy's gaze, his eyes sliding down her body towards the floor. She looked tired, even in her baggy outfit, which was obviously designed for warmth instead of fashion. His eyes stopped at the box in her hands, narrowing slightly, the blood rushing to his ears. Was that...No! His mind was screaming, looking for an alternative, refusing to believe what his eyes were seeing. There, clutched in her hands, for the entire world to see, was a pregnancy test. Jax felt ill. A million thoughts raced through his head. Was she serious? Was this a sick joke? Was it his? Was she going to try saying it was his? What was he going to do? There was no way that Jax could be a father, could he? More importantly, did he want to be? He wasn't sure he had an answer for that question just yet, maybe he never would. He knew that he couldn't do this though, he couldn't pretend that he hadn't seen the test. Why hadn't she told him? Unless it wasn't his? Maybe that was why she wasn't too upset that he had played her, that he had been a jerk with her, because she had someone else to comfort her, someone else to fall back on. As soon as the thought entered his head, Jax dismissed it. Cassidy didn't seem like the type of person who would have a string of lovers waiting, in fact, she didn't even seem like the type of person who would have sex outside of a committed relationship. Yet here she was.

Jax felt as if he had been standing there forever, just staring at Cassidy's pregnancy test, instead of the mere moments that it had actually been. With a monumental effort, he dragged his eyes back upwards, and looked at Cassidy's face. She looked tired, sick. Guilt stabbed at him, he was better than this, this was not who he was, not really.

"Cassidy, it's nice to see you again, this is Carmen," he nodded towards the woman at his side.

"Cassidy? It's nice to meet you," Carmen smiled openly. "I didn't realise the two of you knew each other."

"Cassidy works at the front office at the school where I used to teach last year," Jax

53

supplied quickly, not wanting to give Cassidy a chance to tell Carmen how she really knew him.

"Oh, I bet you'd have some stories to tell, wouldn't you?"

"My lips are sealed." Although Cassidy answered Carmen's question, it was Jax that she spoke to. "Well, I'd better-" Cassidy made to move, waving the hand that held the pregnancy test in some kind of weird goodbye salute.

"Oh, my gosh!" Carmen squealed. "You're pregnant?" If it was possible for someone to die of embarrassment, it would be Cassidy, right here right now, her face had gone a terrifying shade of beetroot.

"Um, I'm not sure..." Cassidy trailed off.

"But you think you are, don't you? Oh, how wonderful, a baby, that's the most precious thing ever!" Carmen clasped her hands together in front of her chest, a dreamy look on her face. "Oh, I absolutely can't wait to have a baby, I'm so clucky it's not even funny, both of my sisters just recently had babies, my eldest sister had a baby girl, oh man she is so cute, and my youngest sister just had twins. Honestly, she's so lucky," Carmen shook her head in disbelief. "Twin boys, also the cutest things ever. Honestly, I just can't wait until I have a baby growing inside of me, it's literally the only thing I want in life now."

"Maybe you should put those back then," Cassidy gestured towards the ridiculously large container of condoms in Jax's hands, the ghost of a smile on her lips.

"True," Carmen laughed, "but they aren't for us, I mean, they are, but we intend to use them in an entirely different manner than what their original purpose is," she leant towards Cassidy conspiratorially, "Jax and I are planning on making a penis sculpture for a friend's birthday, made out of tiny plaster condoms. We'll just fill these up and once they are set, cut them out of the latex, and then use more plaster to bind the entire thing together, hopefully, it works out."

"It sounds really funny, hopefully, it works out for you. Well, I better go, it was nice to meet you, Carmen," Cassidy nodded before turning and walking away towards the checkout without a second glance at Jax. Jax was torn, he wanted to follow Cassidy, he had a million questions he wanted to ask her, but on the other hand, he didn't want Carmen asking him a million questions about who Cassidy was and why he was going after her. In the end, he did nothing, merely stayed with Carmen while she added a bunch of bandages to his arms before they checked out. The longer he was out in town with Carmen, the longer Jax had to let his behaviour towards Cassidy stew and fester.

He had been a jerk, worse even, because he had acted with deliberate intent. Urgh, what was wrong with him? He should ever have introduced Cassidy to Carmen as a mere acquaintance, he knew that, but what could he have said? This is Cassidy, the girl I had a fling with over Easter? This is Cassidy, kind of a friend with benefits but not really? No, of course not, that would have been even worse. He should have introduced her as a co-worker, that at least was technically true. Jax didn't miss the hurt in her eyes when he had dismissed her so easily. Jax sighed heavily, he knew what he had to do. As soon as Carmen had finished with her purchases, he made his excuses, feigning a migraine, and dropping her straight home. Once he left her place, he drove the most logical route from town to Cassidy's house, hoping that he wasn't too late to catch her, knowing that she would have walked, remembering from their time working together that she didn't drive. As he rounded the corner, he spied her just up ahead and quickly pulled up alongside her.

"Cassidy, hey, wait, can I give you a lift?"

CHAPTER SIX - CASSIDY

Cassidy stopped and stared at Jax sitting in his car. Was he for real? Shaking her head slowly, she started to walk again, only stopping when Jax had the audacity to honk his horn at her.

"What the hell?" She rounded on him. "Do I look like a dog to you? You can't just go around beeping your horn at people, Jax. Disgusting!" Cassidy stormed off, walking faster than usual, fuelled by anger and annoyance. She watched Jax drive past her and pull off the road up ahead, park his car and get out. Head held high, Cassidy had every intention of waltzing straight past the arrogant jerk, and she would have to, if only he hadn't reached out and grabbed her arm to stop her.

"What?" She hissed.

"Would you just stop for a minute please, so that I can talk to you?"

"I have nothing to say to you."

"Then maybe you can listen, honey, because I sure as hell have plenty to say to you."

"You know what, Jax? Screw you!" Cassidy spat out, again heading for home.

The last thing wanted was to talk to Jax right now. By the time she got to the end of the next street, she was relieved to see that Jax had given up and was nowhere in sight. Good. Cassidy slowed her steps, sucking in a deep lungful of air. Her shoulders slumping. She couldn't even begin to process everything that had happened already today, she didn't know where to start. A tear trickled slowly down her face, and she brushed it away impatiently, blinking rapidly to try and stop any more from following suit. She was not going to cry, not over him, not anymore. Her words were pointless and the tears continued to fall. She wasn't even sure why she was crying, not really, it wasn't as if Jax's reaction had been unexpected, it was just that Cassidy had hoped for more, so much more. She couldn't believe that he was back in town, why hadn't he told her? It was obvious that he hadn't wanted her to know, but to introduce her to his new squeeze like that, that was just plain cruel. Cassidy was angry that she had been right, she knew that Jax had been avoiding her, she just knew it. It didn't matter though, did it? She had still hoped that she had been wrong, she had still hoped that he hadn't just used her, that there had been some kind of connection, no matter how stupid that sounded. She was an optimist, she couldn't help it, she just wanted everything to turn out for everybody.

The only good thing to have come from all of this was that she hadn't told anybody. She would have been beyond mortified had anybody known that she had thrown herself at Jax, willingly, and then he had just thrown her away like trash. Gah, she had been so stupid, so very, very stupid, and now look where it had gotten her. She should have just kept her mouth shut. She should never have written Jax that letter in the first place, that is what started the whole thing. If she had never sent the letter, then when he had spoken to her in the supermarket, she would merely have said hello and walked away, she would never have agreed to coffee. She wouldn't have been flattered, she wouldn't have thought that he had read the letter but hadn't responded because he had been shy, and most importantly, she wouldn't have let her imagination run away with her. She wouldn't have read more into Jax's smile, she wouldn't have allowed herself to believe that he was smiling at her because he liked her, because he thought she was something special, instead she would have seen the truth, that he was smiling at her because he was a nice person who smiled at everyone. No, she should never have told him how she felt about him it had been the catalyst for everything and her downfall.

Cassidy spent the rest of the walk home assuring up her defences, building the walls around her heart that little bit higher, that little bit sicker, fixing up all the cracks that the light had dared to push through during these past few weeks. Cassidy was a professional at guarding her emotions, usually, this was just one tiny slip, that's all, nothing major, tomorrow she could start new, she would go back to being cold and aloof, safe. A coldness started to creep into Cassidy's bones as the realisation of losing Jax became a reality. It was so much worse this time around, because, unlike last time when he was just moving to Brisbane, this time he had been hers, even if only for a short while, and now she had lost him. It was so silly really, the sheer weight of grief that she carried with her. Even if she had someone to confide in, she knew they wouldn't understand her, she loved big, that's what she did, that was who she was, she didn't do things small, or by halves, or casually. She was unlike all the other women she knew, she could never just have a fling, emotions were always involved, at least for her.

One of the most painful things for Cassidy was just how happy Jax had looked in the chemist. He hadn't looked embarrassed or uncomfortable or ashamed at being caught with another woman at all. Is this why he had stopped returning her calls? Another uncomfortable thought occurred to Cassidy, just how long had Jax been seeing this woman, she was obviously a local, after all, she had spoken about them having a mutual friend. Was she the woman that he was dating before he left for Brisbane? Have they been dating this whole time? Oh no! Cassidy was dismayed to think that she could actually have been the other woman in this situation, what a mess. Thank goodness she had never told Jax how she truly felt about him, she would rather die than confess how she felt about Jax, she loved him, and she was in love with him. She couldn't even begin to imagine what she would do if the pregnancy test was in fact positive. Cassidy had never imagined herself having children she didn't know the first thing about being a mother, and she certainly never had any role models to guide her.

By the time Cassidy got home, she was hot, tired, and decidedly nauseous, her apprehension levels shooting through the roof at the sight of Jax's car parked by the curb outside her house. Apparently, he hadn't got the message after all.

CHAPTER SEVEN - JAX

"Cassidy, did you have a nice walk?" Jax greeted her as she walked through her front gate.

"Go to hell!" Cassidy muttered as she headed for her front door.

"No thanks, I'm not interested." Jax watched as Cassidy unlocked her front door and stepped through, moving to close it behind her, but Jax was too quick for her, shoving his foot in the door jamb to prevent the door from closing.

"Seriously?" Cassidy arched her eyebrows at him. "Move your foot, Jax," she commanded.

"I just want to talk, Cassidy, that's all."

"Ha! So, I guess it's all about you and what you want, isn't it, Jax?" Her eyebrow arched at him.

"Really? I seem to recall you getting quite a lot of what you enjoyed as well," Jax watched as Cassidy paled.

"What do you want, Jax?" She asked quietly, her eyes avoiding his.

"I told you, I just want to talk, that's all."

"Fine," she crossed her arms over her chest, "go ahead, I'm listening."

"Aren't you going to invite me in Cassidy?" Jax prompted.

"No," Cassidy's voice was firm.

"Cassidy, please?" Jax tried again.

"No, Jax. This is my house, my space, and I don't want you in it."

"Okay, fair enough, will keep will you at least sit out on the front patio with me, please, so that I'm not standing here talking to the door?"

"Fine," Cassidy sighed, "but I need a minute first." She shut the door in his face. Jax made himself comfortable on one of the patio chairs and waited for her to return. She didn't keep him waiting long, reappearing after only a few minutes, a box of salty crackers and a bottle of water tucked under her arm. As Cassidy flopped down in the chair opposite him in started snacking away at her crackers, Jax raised an eyebrow, but wisely said nothing.

"Well," she glowered at him, "talk."

"I saw what you purchased at the chemist Cassidy," Jax got right to the point.

"So," she shrugged, "I saw what you and your new girlfriend were buying too."

"My new girlfriend? I wasn't aware that I had an old girlfriend." The barb hit as it was supposed to, Cassidy sucking in a sharp breath. "Are you pregnant?"

"I don't know," Cassidy spoke after a pause.

"But you think you are?" Jax probed.

"Possibly, my period is late," Cassidy sat the box of crackers aside and took a large swig of her water. "Also, I haven't been feeling very well the past couple of days, nauseous, headache, that kind of thing."

"I see," Jax nodded.

"No, you don't," Cassidy shook her head. "My period is never late, Jax, never."

"How late are you?"

"Five days."

"Sheesh," he sighed.

"Aren't you going to ask me if the baby is yours?" Cassidy questioned frostily.

"No," he lied.

"Liar," she accused. "I can see it written all over your face."

"Okay, fine Cassidy. Is it mine, hey, is that what you want me to say?" Jax let his annoyance show through.

"If that's what you think, then yes, I want you to say it," Cassidy bit back.

"I don't know what to think, Cassidy, honestly, we hooked up for one night, we text each other occasionally, a few random phone calls, we're kind of friends, yet you don't even tell me that you think you might be pregnant," Jax fumed. "I'm the supposed possible father, and yet you don't even tell me. What am I supposed to think?" He ran his hand through his hair.

"Maybe if you hadn't been such an ass," Cassidy seethed, "maybe if you had actually answered the phone when I rang you, instead of always gaslighting me, then maybe I would have been able to tell you," she spat out, her voice thick with unshed tears. Great, now he had made her cry, urgh!

"Cassidy," he sighed, "I wish I had an excuse, but I don't, I'm sorry."

"No," she waved his apology away, wiping her eyes, "it's fine, I'm too intense, too exhausting to be friends with," she laughed self-deprecatingly. Jax wondered who had hurt her in the past for her to actually believe that. "Besides," she continued, "you were right. We were never anything. I was the pathetic woman who had a crush on you for way too long, and you were the popular man who never saw me, in fact, I doubt you even knew that I existed for most of the years that I have known you," she shrugged. "Honestly, we both know that the only reason we ever ended up together was simply that you needed some fun for the night, and I happened to be walking past at the time. It could have been anyone, Jax, seriously, it was just bad luck that it happened to be me." Jax wasn't entirely sure how he felt about Cassidy calling what they had shared together bad luck but decided not to comment on it.

"You were there, Cassidy, convenient, that part is true, I'm not going to lie, but let me make two things very clear. One, despite what you might think of me, I do not make it a habit to go sleeping around, there is generally some kind of mutual relationship in place first, and two, you're wrong. I knew you existed, of course, I did."

"Fine." By the way that she snorted at his last comments, he knew that Cassidy didn't believe him. Jax decided to let it go for now.

"So," Jax cleared his throat, "will you do the test now?"

"No," Cassidy shook her head, and he felt a stab of disappointment.

"Because I'm here?" He guessed.

"No," Cassidy clarified, "because the box says to do it first thing in the morning."

"Oh." He wondered if she would let him come back tomorrow, to wait while she did the test? It was unlikely, she would probably only accuse him of not trusting her to do the test, of checking up on her. "Would you, ah, like me to...I mean, if you want, I can come over first thing in the morning, um, sit with you while you do the test."

"You want to watch me pee on a stick?" Cassidy sounded incredulous. "Oh!" She exclaimed suddenly, shaking her head as if confused. "Sorry, of course, I didn't think, but obviously you want to know as soon as possible, especially Carmen I would imagine," Cassidy prattled on.

"Carmen?" Jax spoke over the top of Cassidy. "What does she have to do with anything?"

"What does she have to...Jax, I hope you're joking right now. You heard her, she is desperate to have a baby, chances are she's feeling pretty hurt and betrayed right about now...Oh. You didn't tell her, did you?" Cassidy's mouth flattened into a line.

"Tell her?" Jax was utterly confused.

"That I might be pregnant," Cassidy supplied.

"No," Jax shook his head, "why would I?"

"Oh, I don't know, Jax, maybe because you are dating, because you cheated on her," Cassidy huffed. At this, Jax broke into a laugh, no wonder Cassidy had been so keen to avoid his gaze in the chemist.

"There seems to be a bit of a misunderstanding here, Cassidy. I'm not dating Carmen, I never have, she's my best mate's girl, we're friends, that's all."

"Oh." Cassidy nodded.

"Oh indeed," Jax agreed. So, Cassidy had thought he had cheated on someone else, with her. She must really have such a low opinion of him now. Still, on the plus side, she had thought about him, and had acted almost jealous. Huh, maybe she didn't hate him quite as much as she pretended to?

"I get up pretty early," Cassidy spoke suddenly.

"Okay." Jax nodded.

"I mean, really early, Jax," Cassidy emphasised.

"I understand," Jax smiled.

"If you were to get here by, say, five o'clock tomorrow morning, you could wait while I do the test."

"Thank you."

"It's fine," she stated simply. Jax had the feeling that she would say that regardless of if it was true or not. Jax was conflicted. He had the strange urge to stay, not for his own needs, but for Cassidy, to just simply sit in silence and provide companionship. He knew she wouldn't welcome that though, least of all from him, so instead, he stood reluctantly, and took his leave, heading back to the room he was currently occupying at his friend's house, to spend the rest of the day sitting on the edge of his bed, thinking.

CHAPTER EIGHT - CASSIDY

True to her word, the following day Cassidy was up bright and early, in fact, by the time that Jax arrived at her house, she had already been up for several hours.

Cassidy opened the front door, then stood back and waited for Jax to enter. Apart from picking her up and dropping her off to go to the festival, and then his visit yesterday, Jax had never been to Cassidy's house, and she found herself oddly self-conscious.

"Hi, come in, sit anywhere," she waved her arm around the general direction of the lounge room. "I'll just, um, you know, go do the test," she stuttered awkwardly as Jax sat down, nodding at her. Cassidy had been doing nothing all morning except drinking glasses full of water, and she was more than ready to administer the test. She followed the directions carefully, the very last thing she wanted was to get a false result, in any direction, and then sat the test on the window ledge. Cassidy took her time washing her hands, hoping to use up as much of the two minutes required for the test result to show as possible, trying not to let her nerves get the better of her.

Eventually, Cassidy turned the bathroom tap off and sat on the edge of the bathtub, to wait for the rest of the time to pass. When the alarm on Cassidy's phone finally went off, alerting her to the fact that the test was ready to be read, she jumped up, both desperate to see the result and actually terrified. She wiped her shaking hands on the side of her pants before shakily picking up the pregnancy test. With a deep breath, she looked down at the test, her heart sinking. The test was positive, Cassidy was pregnant. She let out a breath she didn't realise she had been holding and sat back down on the side of the bathtub. There was a coldness slowly seeping through Cassidy's body, as she blinked furiously, desperate not to cry. She was pregnant, right there in black and white, pregnant. Her, Cassidy, was going to be a mother. What on earth was she going to do? She had never imagined ever having children, it was just something that she had never considered, she never thought it would happen to her, and she wasn't sure that she wanted it to happen to her.

Cassidy knew that she was the last person in the world who should be having a child, especially a child out of wedlock when there wasn't even a man in the picture. Sure, Jax might be in the lounge room right now waiting for her to find out if she was pregnant or not, but she knew how it was. As soon as she told him that she was pregnant, she knew he would go, he would leave, and go back to his normal life and not give her or the baby another thought. Not that that was wrong exactly, especially as this wasn't a planned event, and it wasn't at all surprising to Cassidy, if she was him, she would probably do the same thing. She couldn't be a mum; Cassidy didn't know the first thing about being a mum. None of her friends were mothers, as for her own mother, her biological mother, she had been the worst kind of person. Cassidy had been tormented and neglected her entire life at the hands of her mother, and her father hadn't been any better. The only thing they had ever taught her was that you couldn't trust people, that people always hurt you. That, and the fact that nobody would ever love anybody like Cassidy. That had been her mother's favourite catchphrase.

A number of times every day, no matter what Cassidy did, her mother would always reply by telling her that nobody was ever going to want somebody like her, or that no one could ever love somebody like her. Soon, it had become ingrained in Cassidy. By the time she was a teenager, Cassidy knew she was broken inside, the years of neglect and abuse having taken their toll. She had genuinely believed that nobody would ever be able to fix her, or would ever be able to make things right, or would ever be able to make her whole again. So, she did the only thing that she knew how to do in order to survive, she packed all of her dreams away deep into the darkest depths of her soul and she never spoke of them ever again. Finding somebody to love her, somebody that she could love back, finding somebody to have a family with, a life with, a future that was built on friendship and loyalty and trust and mutual respect, had been her dearest dream when she was younger. It had been years and years since Cassidy had even considered allowing herself to think those things. What a cruel twist of fate that she should now find herself pregnant, and to Jax no less, the one man that she had crushed on for years, the one man that she had built up in her head to be this amazing, compassionate, light-filled, trustworthy, amazing man.

Of course, her mother was right, he didn't want her, and he sure as heck wouldn't want this baby when he knew it existed. Cassidy momentarily thought about lying to him by telling him that she wasn't pregnant, but she knew that she couldn't do that. She wasn't sure what she was going to do yet, but she did know that whatever she decided she would tell Jax, because it was the right thing to do, even if he never wanted to see her again, even if he never wanted anything to do with the baby, it was still the right thing to do, he was still the baby's biological father, and he still had the right to know he or she existed. No matter how much it hurt Cassidy. Cassidy left the pregnancy test on the bathroom sink and returned to the lounge room, Jax jumping up as soon as he saw her enter the room.

"Cassidy?" He asked. She watched as he swallowed rapidly, his Adam's apple bobbing up and down.

"The test was positive," she choked out, "I'm pregnant." With that, Cassidy promptly burst into tears.

CHAPTER NINE - JAX

"You're pregnant," Jax scratched out through a dry throat. Cassidy didn't answer, she couldn't answer, she merely nodded through her tears. The blood pounded in Jax's ears, his insides were in turmoil, he wanted to scream, to swear, to rage, although he knew there was no reason for that, as essentially the blame was entirely his, he should have been more careful. He looked at Cassidy before him, tears streaking down her face, she looked like a wretched mess. He could only imagine what she must be thinking and feeling right now. Panic and uncertainty welled up inside of him, he wished he could run, flee, go anywhere but here. Jax had never been in this situation before, heck even though he came from a large family, none of his immediate friends had children yet. He would be the first, he would be the one setting the example for others, for his friends, and ultimately, for his child. Jax had no idea what he could possibly say to Cassidy in order to make the situation any better, so he did the only thing he could think, he crossed the room and pulled her into his arms, holding her close against his chest while she cried, only releasing her once her sobs had subsided into hiccups.

"Do you feel up to talking about this, Cassidy?" He asked as she sat on the couch beside him.

"I don't know," she chewed her lip nervously, not meeting his eyes. "I mean, I'll understand if you want to leave, Jax, I know this was never part of the plan, and it's certainly not something that we ever expected to occur."

"I'm not going anywhere, Cassidy. I know that this wasn't planned, I don't know how you feel about it, or how I even feel about it right now, that is something that we can talk about later if you'd like to, but just so you know, I'm not going anywhere, okay? We are in this together."

"It's okay, Jax, you know I won't blame you if you go," Cassidy replied in a small voice. He wondered what had happened in her life to make her so certain that he was planning on leaving.

"Cassidy, I'm not going anywhere, all right? I don't know what happened in your past to make you so distrustful, but I'm staying," Jax's tone brokered no argument.

"Do you think I should keep the baby?"

"I don't know," he answered truthfully, "I think that we should talk about all of the options, but ultimately, it's your body, it's your choice, and I will support you in whatever you decide, Cassidy."

"I don't...I mean...I never thought about being a mother, it was never something that I planned for my life, I just never really thought about it one way or the other."

"I understand," Jax nodded, "I never imagined I would be a father either, I mean, you know my lifestyle, it's not exactly conducive to raising a family."

"I don't know what to do."

"Well, look Cassidy, we don't have to have all of the answers today, do we? I just...I know...I know that I hurt you when I blew you off in Brisbane, and I'm sorry about that. If I could go back and change things, I would, but I can't. I just want you to know that it was not anything you had done, okay, it was completely me. I just screw up everything that I ever try to do, I just...I want to do the right thing, but I always end up stuffing it up. I just thought that it would be easier with you if I simply stopped returning your calls, I'm sorry, I never wanted to hurt you, that was why I stopped returning your calls, to save you from the trainwreck that is my life."

"I didn't have the best childhood, Jax, I'm not sure that I know how to be a mother, I don't know if emotionally I can be there for a child, I don't know if I could love a child." Her confession was stilted, it was obvious that it pained her to have to admit it.

"Well," Jax said, "let's talk about it. The way I see it, Cassidy, we have three options. Option one, we terminate the pregnancy, option two, we proceed with the pregnancy and put the child up for adoption, or, option three, we proceed with the pregnancy and we raise the child, together."

"I don't think that I could carry a baby, deliver the baby, and then put it up for adoption, Jax, I just don't think I could do that."

"Well, there you go, see, we've already ruled that option out, so now we only have two left."

"You make it sound so easy."

"Sorry, Cassidy, I'm just I'm trying to make it easier for you, for us."

"I think I'm going to need a few days to decide, Jax, I think I want to go and sleep right now."

"I understand, it's been a shock, for both of us. Is there anything I do, anything I can get for you?"

"Jax," Cassidy looked at him. "Were you serious when you said that you would stay, that we would do this together?"

"Of course, I was serious, you have my word." Jax took his leave soon after, assuring Cassidy that should she need anything all she had to do was call him. He didn't want to return to his friend's house just yet, instead, he decided to drive around Alice Springs for a while, to try clear his head, to think things through. He didn't know where he stood, or how he felt at the moment. He just could not imagine being a father, but then he supposed that most men felt that way when they first discovered that there were going to be fathers. Jax had had a wonderful father, truly his best friend. After his death, his mother had remarried, and his stepfather was equally as wonderful, happily taking Jax and his brother and continuing to do all of the activities that he had enjoyed with his father.

His stepfather had never tried to take his father's place, had never tried to supersede him in Jax's affections. He had simply stood in and become Jax's friend. Jax hadn't wanted for role models, his brother was a father twice over, a wonderful, wonderful father. Jax wasn't concerned about if he could do it, he just wasn't sure he wanted to do it. One thing Jax knew for sure was that he wanted to find out where he stood before he went back and spoke to Cassidy again. If he decided that he did not want to be a father, and she decided to keep this child, he wanted to be able to be honest with her about how that would look. There was only one person that Jax trusted enough to give him advice in this matter, and that was his brother, Kyle. Jax pulled his car off to the side of the road and dialled his brother's number, Kyle answering on the third ring.

"Hello. Amy, no, your brother does not want any sultanas, sheesh, honestly, you turn your back for two seconds and suddenly there is a handful of sultanas stuffed in Max's mouth!" Max was Kyle's six-month-old son, a brother to three-year-old Amy, who doted on him.

"Is this a bad time?" Jax asked.

"No, no, it's fine," his brother insisted, "to what do I owe the call?"

"I kinda got myself into a situation here, and I would like some advice."

"Oh, that sounds mysterious," his brother teased.

"There is this is girl," Jax started.

"Urgh, honestly Jax!" His brother interrupted him.

"No, hear me out," Jax continued, "she's pregnant."

"And let me guess, you're the father?"

"Of course, I'm the father, if I wasn't the father, I wouldn't be asking for advice now, would I?"

"So, then, what do you plan to do about it?"

"I don't know, that's why I was calling you, for advice," Jack said sarcastically, completely exasperated by Kyle.

"I'm not going to tell you what you should do, that's not my place, but I will say this, you need to think about this, and you need to be certain, because let me tell you, once a baby comes along, everything changes, and if you're in its life to start with, and then you're not, that's unforgivable."

"I know, I just..." he trailed off.

"Let me ask you this, do you love her?"

"I don't know, we haven't been together that long."

"How long?"

"A weekend," Jax was embarrassed to admit.

"Oh, for goodness' sake Jax!"

"In my defence, we have known each other for a lot longer, ten years or so."

"When are you going to settle down, hey, get married, you know, make a commitment?"

"I don't know if I ever will."

"What are you so concerned about Jax? You know nothing changes when you get married, right? Just look at Jules and me. I still do all the things I used to do before we got married, as does she, only now it's better because I get to come home and share things with her, and get her perspective on things, and talk things over with her. The joy I get from what I do is now doubled because I get to share it, okay, I haven't lost anything in getting married, in falling in love, I've only gained. Now, let me tell you this, neither of our children was planned, not exactly. There was an idea that maybe sometime in the future, perhaps, we might have a child, but nothing definitive. Both were complete accidents.

"You're joking! I had no idea."

"No, why would you? We adore both of our children equally, and at the time, neither of us knew if we were going to be good parents, we didn't even actually know if we wanted to be parents, but the reality was, that it was going to happen whether we were ready or not, so we got ready. I think you're asking yourself the wrong question. The question is no longer whether you want to be a father or not because that's already happened, you are now a father, and even before the baby is born, you are a father. The question is whether you are going to stay and be in that child's life, or go, and leave it to be raised without you. That is the question you need to ask yourself, Jax, that is the question you need to decide."

Jax knew that Kyle was right and once he finished on the phone with him, he turned everything over in his mind, only moving once the light on his dashboard faded to grey. Two days later Jax had his answer, he knew where he stood both mentally and emotionally, and he was ready to let Cassidy know. He had spoken to her each day on the phone since learning that she was pregnant, and he was glad that she had not shut him out. He sent her a quick text message asking if he could pop over and speak with her, and she replied immediately with a yes. When he got to her house, he found her sitting outside on the front patio in the sun, a book in her lap.

"Hi," he greeted as he sat down in the chair opposite her. "I don't want to push or to pry, but I wondered if you had had time to think things through and if you had made any decisions yet?"

"I've done nothing but think about it since you left Jax, but I haven't made any decisions, nor would I, not without you."

"I've been doing some thinking too, and I've decided that if you want to keep this child, then I would like to be involved. Not in a part-time weekend dad kind of way, but in a full-time every day there for the big and for the little thing's kind of way."

"What exactly are you saying, Jax?"

"If you decide to keep the baby, I would like to co-parent with you," he stated.

"Co-parent?" Cassidy sounded confused.

"Yes, co-parent."

"How would that work? What would that look like, exactly?"

"Ideally, we would live in the same town, perhaps the same house. I would be free to come and go, as would you. All decisions would be made together, we would share our lives together, kind of like roommates with a baby," he explained.

"Roommates with the baby? That seems like a very big commitment for you to make Jax, Are you sure about this?"

"I'm one hundred percent certain. If you go ahead with this pregnancy, I want to be involved every single day, every step of the way. No child of mine will ever wonder who their dad, is or what they are like. Now, tell me, what have you been thinking?"

"Well, I can't have a termination Jax, I just can't do it."

"I understand," he nodded. "So then, we're having a baby?"

"I don't know how good I'll be with this Jax, I didn't have role models the way you did, but yes," she smiled fleetingly, "we're having a baby."

CHAPTER TEN - CASSIDY

"Would you come to New South Wales with me, Cassidy? I promised to visit my parents these holidays, and I think it would be nice for them to meet you." Jax and Cassidy were currently sitting on Cassidy's front patio, enjoying the last of the day's sunshine. It had been a week since they had decided to keep the baby, and they had settled easily into a routine of sorts. Jax called Cassidy on the telephone every morning and she called him every evening. They had also spent time together each day, simply sitting together, talking about mundane, easy topics, and building a rapport. True to his word, Jax had treated Cassidy as one would treat a roommate, with friendship and platonic affection. While Cassidy had been grateful at first, she had quickly become disappointed and irritated at the ease with which Jax had seemingly switched off all attraction for her. She was angry with herself as well, why should she care if he lusted after her or not, it wasn't as if she was still lusting after him, was it? No, she had to face facts. She was

88

pregnant now, and any hope that she still had of having a relationship, with anyone, was now out of the question. Even if her body somehow magically stayed the same, she would have the responsibility of a child, she wouldn't be able to drop everything to go out on a date.

"I don't know...How long would we be gone for?" She pulled herself out of her thoughts to answer his question.

"Two weeks. I'd like to leave tomorrow."

"Tomorrow? Um," she thought about his question. There really was no reason for her to say no, it wasn't as if she had anything better to do, but then again, she wasn't sure that she should say yes either. It seemed like she might be setting herself up for heartache. Cassidy hadn't actually thought too much about it, but presumably, as Jax's parents, they would expect to be involved in the baby's life in some way. She wondered what they were like. Would they be surprised that Jax was going to be a father? Happy about it? Cassidy didn't have any family to speak of, the only people she would share the news with would be a couple of friends, and maybe work at some point. "Okay," Cassidy tried not to sigh, there really was no reason to deny Jax his request, "I'll come with you and meet your family, what time do you want to leave?"

"As early as possible, Cassidy, do you think you could be ready to leave just before three o'clock?"

"I'll set the alarm," she smiled, knowing that she would already be awake, being the insomniac that she was. They spent the rest of Jax's visit planning their travel time, debating over how often they would need to stop, and discussing what Cassidy would need to pack. Once Jax left, Cassidy went ahead and packed her suitcase, before setting her alarm and crawling into bed.

The following morning Jax arrived on time and after Cassidy had double-checked that her house was locked up, they set off, swinging past a local drive-thru for some breakfast, which Cassidy later regretted.

"Cass," concern etched Jax's voice, "is there anything I can do?"

"No," Cassidy managed to get out before doubling back over and bringing up more of her breakfast by the side of the road. When she was finally finished, Jax handed her a bottle of water, which she took gratefully, twisting it open and sipping it slowly. It was an act that was repeated several times over the course of the rest of the day, the original travel plan having been thrown out long ago. Instead of only stopping for food and petrol, they had been stopping nearly every hour, until finally, Jax pulled off at a roadside rest stop and turned to look at her, curled up on the front passenger seat, utterly exhausted.

"I think we should spend the night in the next town."

"No, I'm fine," Cassidy protested weakly, "I don't usually get car sick, I'm sure it will settle down."

"Cass, I don't think it's travel sickness," Jax smiled sympathetically at her, "I think it's morning sickness."

"What? No, it can't be, it's been all day," Cassidy frowned. Was that even possible?

"I know," Jax nodded, "my sister-in-law had a horrid time as well, she was sick all day every day for her entire first pregnancy."

"Urgh, if that's the case, you'd better just shoot me, I can't do that."

"I'm not going to shoot you," Jax laughed, "but I can take you to the doctor, just to make sure nothing is wrong."

"I'm sure I'm fine, I don't need to bother a doctor," Cassidy yawned, "seriously, after a good sleep I am sure things will be better." At least, she certainly hoped that they would be. They found a small motel in the next town with a vacancy, and once Jax had checked them in, Cassidy had a long shower and hopped into bed. "Jax?"

"Hmm?" He didn't look up from the apparent blanket mound he was creating on the room's couch.

"What are you doing?"

"I'm making up the couch," he shrugged, "there's only one bed, Cassidy, I just figured...I mean...I thought you would prefer to have it all to yourself so that you can stretch out."

"Oh." She hadn't noticed until now that there was only one bed. That was thoughtful of him, sleeping on the couch. "You don't have to do that, Jax, there is plenty of room, and you need a good night's sleep too, you know."

"Are you sure?" He frowned at her.

"Sure," she shrugged, "I trust you." Cassidy snuggled down as Jax pulled the blankets from the couch and added them to the bed, luxuriating in the added warmth. He climbed in beside her, shifting around until finally falling still.

"Cass?"

"Hmm?"

"I was thinking, let's not tell my parents that you are pregnant just yet, let's wait for a while, maybe tell them in a couple more months, let's just allow them to get to know you first."

"That's fine, Jax, I'm happy to wait until you're ready."

Two days later, they finally drove into Bingara, passing the welcome sign on the bridge. Cassidy tried not to let her nerves get the better of her, she had never met anyone's parents before, what if they didn't like her? She had tried not to let her nerves show, but she suspected that Jax had seen through her false bravado if his constant chatter about his parents loving everyone was any indication. Despite their somewhat shaky start, Jax had shown himself to be a considerate and dependable companion, and Cassidy was finding herself more and more relaxed in his presence. She had gotten over her initial apprehension at his co-parenting suggestion and was relaxed enough with him now to actually start having conversations about their baby, which was surreal for Cassidy, and certainly, something that she had never expected would ever happen to her.

"We're nearly there," Jax spoke up from beside her. Cassidy took the time to peer out of the window at the sleepy little town. With a population of just over fourteen hundred people, Bingara was your typical small Australian town. There were a couple of pubs, a fish and chip shop, a small independent grocery store, a butcher, a newsagent that doubled as a post office, and a bakery.

The main street was lined with orange trees, and the blossoms wafted their scent through the car window and over Cassidy. The smell was divine, and Cassidy closed her eyes and breathed in deeply. As quaint as Bingara was, Cassidy thought it would be hard to live there, it didn't seem rich with opportunity. Jax pulled into the circular driveway of a sprawling house, and beeped his horn twice in quick succession, the front door swung open, and a middle-aged couple dashed down the front steps, headed towards the car. Jax gave Cassidy's hand a quick squeeze before he got out of the car and went to greet his parents. Cassidy followed slowly behind, not wanting to intrude on his parent's time with him. When Jax saw her standing there, he pulled away from his mum and came to stand with her.

"Mum, Tony, I want you to meet Cassidy," he introduced.

"Cassidy, it's so nice to meet you, please, call me Judy," his mother embraced her, hugging her tightly. "This is my husband, Tony."

"Nice to meet you," he shook Cassidy's hand firmly. Cassidy smiled back at Jax's parents, it was obvious that they were curious about her, and she wondered just what, if anything, he had already told them.

Jax picked up their bags and led Cassidy through the spacious house to a large bedroom, featuring a classic farmhouse look.

"Jax, it's gorgeous!"

"Mum will be pleased; she designed the room herself."

"She seems lovely, Jax, when she hugged me before, she really hugged me, you know what I mean?" Cassidy cleared her throat and tried to explain what she was feeling, overwhelmed with the care and affection shown to her by Jax's mum, as if they were old friends. "I didn't expect that, I've never had that."

"Mum has always welcomed everyone brought home as if they were an extension of the family already," Jax crossed the room to pull Cassidy into a hug.

"Just how many girls have you brought home?" Cassidy narrowed her gaze at Jax, suddenly feeling very possessive.

"One, Cassidy. You." A weird warmth spread through Cassidy, and she snuggled against Jax's chest, hoping he didn't notice her blush or wide smile.

Dinner that night was a noisy affair, as well as Cassidy and Jax, his brother Kyle, Kyle's wife Jules, and their two children Max and Amy joined Jax's parents for dinner. Cassidy found herself watched throughout dinner, surreptitiously, by each member of Jax's family. All of them were more than polite and welcoming, but underneath it all, Cassidy sensed confusion, as if they had expected Jax to choose someone else. She couldn't blame them, she didn't think she was what any mother would expect her son to choose, but then again, Jax hadn't chosen her, had he? Fate had played a cruel twist that had forced them together, without the baby, there is no way that Jax would ever have spoken to Cassidy again, she was certain of it. Once Jax told his parents about the baby, they would understand, she was sure of it. Until then, she would just pretend that she didn't notice the glances.

CHAPTER ELEVEN - JAX

When Jax woke up the following morning it was to find Cassidy wrapped around him, her hair splayed out across his chest her breathing soft. Jax smiled at how nice it felt, how natural, to have her sleep in his arms. As Cassidy muttered something in her sleep and shifted against him, Jax was aware that it wasn't just his thoughts that were mindful of Cassidy, every part of his body was just as responsive. He bit back a groan, if this had been a normal relationship, Jax wouldn't hesitate to flip Cassidy over and wake her up in the most delicious ways, but it wasn't, this was a relationship of convenience, and he had given her his word that they would be no more affectionate than roommates, no matter how delicious the memory of Cassidy was, Jax was determined not to cross that line. Staring up at the ceiling, Jax tried to think of anything, everything he could, to stem his arousal. It was to no avail, and frustrated, Jax managed to extricate himself from Cassidy's embrace, and slip unnoticed, into the ensuite, where a warm shower, and the memory of Cassidy, were enough to take care of his immediate issue.

Satisfied, Jax returned to the bedroom and rummaged around in his suitcase to find some clean clothes to wear.

"Morning." A sleepy voice greeted him from behind, and he turned to see Cassidy, half propped up on the pillows.

"Morning yourself," he replied with a smile. "How are you feeling this morning?"

"Okay, I think," her face scrunched up in concentration. "I mean, I haven't done anything yet, and I haven't eaten either, so we'll see what today brings."

"That's a good sign though, right?" He asked, hopeful.

"Yeah, I think so," she shot him a smile. "I'm going to go and have a shower."

"Okay," he watched her legs as they hit the floor, his eyes travelling upwards across the rest of her body. "I'll wait here for you." While Jax waited, he opened his phone and texted his friends to let them know that he had arrived safely in town, their replies coming through quickly. By the time Cassidy had returned from the shower, dressed in a fresh blue sundress, her hair still slightly damp, Jax had made tentative plans for the day.

"How would you feel about going out for the day?" He asked her. "A friend of mine is throwing me a barbecue, and a bunch of my mates are getting together, I thought it might be nice for us both to go."

"I thought the point of coming here was to visit your family?"

"We'll have plenty of time to see them, don't worry, this is just a one-day thing."

"Will it be a late thing?" Cassidy asked as she slid into her sandals.

"Yeah, it'll probably go all day, and most likely half the night," Jax laughed as he remembered past barbecues held at his friend's house. Although they were called barbecues, they were really all-day rages, starting whenever everybody got there, and finishing whenever everybody left. A day full of good food, cold beer, good friends, and great music. What more could you really ask for?

"Okay, Jax, that sounds nice," Cassidy spoke, "as long as your mom and dad didn't have plans first, okay?"

"That seems fair," Jax agreed.

During breakfast with his parents, they discussed their day's plans, thankfully, his parents had yet to make any, they had known that Jax would want to catch up with his friends as well while he was in town. About halfway through breakfast, Cassidy fled the room, hand over her mouth, and didn't return.

"Goodness, is she okay?" Jax's mum asked, concern lacing her voice.

"She had dreadful travel sickness on the way here, Mum, I think she's still just getting over it, I'm sure she'll be fine, I'll go check on her in a minute, okay?" Jax found Cassidy in the ensuite, sitting on the floor, her face resting against the cold wall of the shower.

"Cassidy, are you okay?" Jax knelt beside her.

"I think if I don't move, or eat, or do anything, I'll be okay."

"Come on, let's get you back to bed," Jax helped her to her feet and guided her through to the bedroom, lifting her dress up over her head, despite her feeble protests. He found her nightie in the suitcase and slipped it on over her head, pushing her down onto the mattress, and covering her with the blanket.

"You stay here, I'll go make you some tea." Jax returned a short time later, carrying a tray laden down with tea, bottled water, and salty crackers, placing it on the bedside table so that Cassidy could reach it.

"Jax, you don't have to stay and look after me, I'll be fine." Cassidy tried to protest.

"Don't be silly, it's my pleasure to look after you."

"No, seriously, I'm probably just going to sleep most of the day, anyway. You're only in town for a short time, you should go and meet up with your friends." She insisted.

"Cassidy, you're not well," Jax frowned at her.

"I know, but you should go anyway. Seriously, you don't know how long it will be before you can get back down here."

"Cassidy, are you sure about this?"

"Yes," she nodded her head. After making sure that Cassidy was certain, Jax agreed that he would go and meet with his friends. He told his parents of their updated plans and assured them that Cassidy would call them if she needed anything at all, and with a final check-in with Cassidy, he left for his friend's house.

By the time Jax arrived, the barbecue was in full swing, his friends all greeting him with a cheer, and he was glad that he had made the choice to come after all.

"Jax, I was starting to think you were going to blow me off," a tall blonde slapped him on the shoulder.

"Sorry, Mark, Cassidy wasn't feeling well, and I hated to leave her alone."

"Who?" Mark's eyebrows knitted together in confusion.

"Cassidy, my...Actually, you know what, it doesn't matter," Jax brushed his friend's question aside, he didn't really feel like going into the entire story right now, it would keep for another time, another day. "I need a beer, how about you?"

"Heck, yeah!" Mark led Jax in the direction of the beer fridge, grabbing two cans and throwing him one. "Now it's a party!" Jax cracked open the can and lifted it to his lips, letting the amber liquid flow down his throat. No sooner had his lips touched the can than he felt a pair of arms snake around his torso and an all too familiar voice rang out in his ears.

"Jaxxy,   I   was   hoping   you would...come...today."

"Tara," he stiffened at the use of her nickname for him, carefully removing her arms

103

from his body. "Considering this shindig is in my honour, I'm surprised to see you here." The very last person Jax had ever wanted to see again was Tara. He had been stupid to get involved with her in the first place, he knew that now. A groupie for his band, she had seemed nice enough, a bit of fun whenever he had been passing through town, nothing serious, or so he had thought. She had thought that she was his muse and had been surprised when he had written something without her being involved in the process. He had been relieved, the fight that had followed had resulted in the end of their relationship. Sadly, for Tara, it had also resulted in an arrest and court case as she had proceeded to stalk him. A few nights after their break up she had taken things too far and had followed his car, running it off the road and into a tree. Jax hadn't been driving at the time, his mother had, and it had been lucky that she had only sustained minor lacerations to her face, and nothing more serious.

"I told Ben not to invite her, that you'd be livid, but, apparently," Mark eyed them both from the top of his own beer, shuffling his feet, "Ben's dating her sister now, so we are supposed to give her a pass."

"Not going to happen," Jax spat out, before nodding at Mark and walking off. Screw Ben and his new girlfriend, Jax wasn't just going to stand around having a chitchat with the person who was responsible for his mother no longer feeling confident enough to drive. Urgh! This was one of the main reasons he avoided relationships, you just can't trust people, you think you know them and then wham! They change. Jax spent the rest of the day drinking and playing the guitar with his mates, ignoring Tara and her every attempt to talk to him. With the exception of Tara, the day had been as good as he remembered them being in the past, and it was with reluctance that he made his excuses to leave, wanting to check on Cassidy and make sure that she was feeling better.

"Jax, you can do that thing, with the keysh," Mark slurred.

"Drive?" Tara supplied.

"Yesh, drive, you can do it, you too drunk," Mark hiccupped, sending the group of friends into fits of laughter.

"So, are you," huffed Tara, "in fact, it would appear that I am the only sober one here tonight. Great, I guess you all expect me to be your designated driver?" With an exaggerated huff, Tara went and fetched her bag, returning and jiggling her keys in the air as if they were all dogs.

"Come on then, whoever wants a lift home better get in the car." Jax would have preferred to walk home, but right now he was having trouble remembering where exactly his parent's house was, and although he knew he had his phone with him somewhere, it had appeared to have gone missing.

With a resigned sigh, he followed her on wobbly feet to her car, all but falling into the front passenger seat, three more partygoers stumbling onto the back seat. The passing scenery made his head spin, so Jax closed his eyes briefly, only opening them once Tara had pulled the car over.

"Ah, here I live," he slurred, frowning at the car door. After watching him try unsuccessfully to open his door, Tara got out of the car and walked around to his side, muttering under her breath about drunks and what she thought of them, yanking the door open and helping him to stand.

"Do you think you could possibly make it to the front door without help?" She asked him sarcastically, and as much as Jax wanted to laugh at her, to remind her that only a few hours ago she was all over him, he resisted, realising that, actually, he most likely would need her help.

"You know, Jax, this is not how I imagined my evening would turn out," she pulled his arm across her shoulders and started to half lead, half drag him up the path to the front door, much to the amusement of the rest of the passengers in the back of the car.

"Oops!" Jax tripped on the edge of the path, his foot catching on the edge of his mother's flower bed, his world tilting dangerously sideways. He grabbed at Tara for support, pulling them both down, as he landed in the violets with a loud thud, Tara sprawled out on top of him.

"Well," she pushed herself up off Jax's chest, still straddling his waist, a wicked gleam in her eyes, "this is much better," she purred, fanning her hands out over his chest.

"What the heck?!" Without warning Jax found himself trapped in a floodlight and he squinted, trying to make out the hazy shadows looking down on him. He watched, fascinated, as the shadows moved around him, familiar, comforting.

One of them stood back and kept their distance. As his eyes grew accustomed to the light, he saw what had made that shadow, his stomach sinking at the sight. Cassidy.

CHAPTER TWELVE - CASSIDY

By late that afternoon Cassidy had finally started to feel a little bit better, she had even managed to keep down a little dinner, much to Judy's delight. She had hoped Jax wouldn't be out long, and by the conversation that she had overheard between Judy and Tony, so had they.

"I just think it is disrespectful, seriously!"

"I know love, but you heard what he said, Cassidy encouraged him to go, it's been ages since he caught up with everyone."

"I not saying that he shouldn't have gone, Tony, but to be gone all day? It's after eight o'clock, and he's left Cassidy here all day, essentially with strangers, when she's not well. I mean, come on, look at her, anyone can tell that she is still ill. It's just plain rude, Tony, honestly, I just do not understand him at times." Moving away from their conversation quietly, so as not to be caught listening in, Cassidy returned to the bedroom and crawled back into bed. If she was being honest, she had also thought that Jax would have been back by now, still, she had told him to go, she just hoped that he was having fun.

Cassidy sat bolt upright, disorientated, not sure what had woken her. Ears straining, she heard a car door slam, followed shortly after by an ominous thud and the sound of someone cursing. Leaving her bed, Cassidy crossed to the door and peered out, both Judy and Tony were already ahead of her, walking towards the front door, and she slipped in behind them, too curious to stay put. Tony turned on the outside porch light and opened the door, Judy gasping, her hand flying to her mouth. Cassidy's eyes grew round, she couldn't believe what she was seeing. There, lying in a bed of flowers, was Jax, grinning up at them, not the least bit ashamed of being caught. Straddling his hips, her hands fanned out over his chest, was one of the most beautiful women Cassidy had ever seen. Model thin, with tresses of lush blonde hair cascading down her back in waves, perfectly pouty lips curved into a smirk, she looked like she could grace the cover of any magazine. With her dress hiked up to her hips, it was clear that they had just interrupted something between the two of them. So, this was why Jax had been home so late, because of her. Cassidy felt ill, a feeling that had nothing to do with the baby.

"What the heck?!" Judy screeched. "Jax, get off my violets, now!" She commanded. "As for you," she snarled at the other woman, "get off my property before I call the police and have you arrested for trespassing." Tony moved to help the other woman clamber off Jax, once she was up, she straightened her dress, blew Jax a kiss, and sauntered off down the path to the curb, before getting in her car and driving off. With a resigned sigh, Tony turned to help Jax up out of the violets, Cassidy's eyes couldn't help but trail down his body, traitors that they were, her mouth hanging open at the sight of Jax's obvious bulge in his pants. Humiliation burned her cheeks. Jax had wanted that other woman, while Cassidy had been right here, sleeping, he had wanted that other woman, more than that, he was going to have her, had they not been interrupted. As Tony led Jax past Judy and Cassidy, Jax suddenly lurched towards Cassidy, grabbing her by the upper arms and winking.

"Shweetheart, help us out, would ya?" He grinned at her, gesturing towards his erection. In the shouting that erupted, Cassidy fled, running down the hall and into the bedroom, slamming the door behind her, locking it with a loud clunk.

She could hear Judy and Tony yelling at Jax from here but couldn't muster any sympathy for him. He had brought this upon himself. How could he do that, to her? It was bad enough that she had noticed his erection, that he was aroused by that other woman, but to go and point it out to his parents? Cassidy had intended to simply ignore it, not wanting to further embarrass herself or Jax, but now...She felt like a common whore. Her cheeks flamed with mortification, what must his parents think of her? What about Jax? He must have a pretty low opinion of her, to ask her such a thing in front of other people, it was beyond disrespectful. Cassidy felt ill, a coldness was spreading throughout her body, and her stomach was full of dread. She should never have agreed to come here with Jax, maybe then she would still be able to pretend that everything was okay, that everything would be fine, that everything would work out. Is this how Jax wanted things to be? Is this what he meant when he said they would co-parent as roommates? Did he expect her to be okay with

112

him bringing home any number of different women, did he think she would do the same with men she met?

Dismayed, Cassidy knew that she should have asked him, she shouldn't have just accepted his idea at face value, she shouldn't have been so keen to keep Jax in her life. She knew now what she had always known, what she had never wanted to admit, not even to herself. She loved Jax and had for a long time, but she knew that he didn't feel the same way about her. In fact, Cassidy knew that not only did Jax not love her, but she was pretty sure that he also wasn't that interested in getting to know her, in forming any sort of relationship with her. Why had he offered to co-parent with her? Did he want a baby that much? Maybe he didn't want the responsibility, the hassle of caring for a baby? Was that what she would be, primary caregiver, while he got to do all the fun things, essentially a nanny? Every time she closed her eyes, Cassidy saw that woman straddling Jax, and she knew that despite what she had agreed to while they were in Alice Springs, there was no way that she would be able to co-parent with Jax. She could not live in the same house as him, raising his baby, watching while he continued to live without her, bringing women home, having fun, living his best life while excluding her, while keeping her close enough to torment. The thought of enduring that had Cassidy in tears, and she swiped them away angrily.

She could rant and rave and blame Jax all she liked, but the truth was, this was all her own fault, no one else was to blame. She had gotten her hopes up too high, yet again, she had let her dreams and imagination sweep her away, she had built Jax up, had built their relationship up, into something it wasn't, into something it wasn't meant to be. She was so stupid, so foolish, to trust him, to think that maybe, just maybe, things would be different, things would go her way this time. She should have known better, she should never have listened to her heart, after all, her head was always right, her head protected her, her head knew that people like Jax never ended up with people like her, no matter what the circumstances. Well, she had certainly learnt her lesson, that was for sure, and now she would pay the ultimate price, she would spend the rest of her life raising a child, she only hoped that she didn't stuff it up, that she could raise them better than she had been raised. It was with a heavy heart that Cassidy climbed back into bed, tossing and turning until she finally fell into a fitful sleep.

CHAPTER THIRTEEN - JAX

When Jax woke the following day, his head was pounding, and he felt as if he had swallowed cotton balls. He could hear the buzz of conversation floating around, and, with a mammoth effort, managed to crack one eye open. Huh. He was sprawled, fully clothed, across the couch in the lounge room. Wait, why was he on the couch in the lounge room, where was Cassidy? He hauled himself into a sitting position and looked around. He felt like trash. With a sigh, he heaved himself off the couch and went in search of Cassidy, surprised to find the bedroom door locked.

"Cassidy," he knocked, "Cassidy?"

"Jax," his stepdad appeared in the hallway, "come to the kitchen, your mum has breakfast ready, Cassidy will be down soon, I'm sure." Tony all but propelled Jax into the kitchen, his mother glaring at him when he arrived. Jax was getting the distinct impression that he had somehow offended them. As he was about to open his mouth and ask about it, Cassidy entered the room, dark circles under her eyes,

116

her lips pressing into a thin line when she caught sight of him already seated at the table. His mother rushed to the table, shooing Cassidy into the seat opposite him, and placing a large plate of pancakes on the table, followed by another of bacon and eggs. As she went back for the toast, the back door swung open, and Kyle, Jules, Max and Amy barrelled through to the kitchen.

"Jax," his brother clapped him on the shoulder, "I hear you had quite the eventful night, have you two made up yet?" He waggled his eyebrows in the direction of Cassidy, whose head was down, her eyes fixed firmly towards the tabletop. Great. He had done something wrong. Whatever it was, it must have been pretty intense, considering his brother was the only one bothering to talk to him.

"Cassidy," he heard his mother's sharp intake of breath, saw the way Cassidy flinched when he said her name. "You're looking better today, a full plate, I see your appetite's returned..." he trailed off as four sets of eyes turned to glare at him. "I thought after breakfast we could-"

"Jax," his brother interrupted him, "shut up." With that, Cassidy stood, her chair scraping against the tiles on the floor, and, without a word or a glance at anyone, left the room, her plate of food untouched.

"Will someone tell me what the heck I'm supposed to have done?" Jax roared, fed up with everyone giving him the stink eye.

"You don't remember?" Kyle asked, incredulous. Jax shrugged and shook his head. "Right, come with me, I'll fill you in on the way to pick up your car."

"Okay," Jax stood to follow his brother, "wait, where's my car?"

"So, you really don't remember anything that happened last night?" Kyle asked him once they were on their way.

"No," Jax stated, wishing that he did.

"Okay, listen, I know you're not married to Cassidy, or seem to have any kind of commitment to her, but mum and dad don't know that, and you were a pretty big jerk to her last night. It was pretty late when you got home, after midnight, and you, ah, were pretty drunk."

"Kyle, please, just tell me," Jax was tired of not knowing.

"Tara brought you home." Jax's head shot around to look at his brother.

"Tara? Oh no, I remember, she was at the party," Jax rubbed his hands over his face as images started to filter through. "Mum must have loved that."

"Yeah, well, there's more. The three of them found you, apparently, you were being rather loud. You were lying in mum's flowers, with Tara straddling you."

"No!" The blood left Jax's face, that couldn't be true, could it? There was no way he would get close enough to Tara for that to happen.

"When Tony pulled Tara off you, you were pretty aroused, you, ah, you asked Cassidy to take care of it for you," Kyle finished awkwardly.

"No, I didn't?!" If Jax had felt uneasy before, he felt positively ill now. Tara had been straddling him? All his memories started to swirl around in his head, snippets of Tara, watching, whispering, driving him home, leaning on her to walk, falling into the flowers, the light, being caught, seeing Cassidy, an overwhelming kaleidoscope of memories and sounds.

"Look, Jax, I know you aren't committed to her at all, but for Pete's sake, she is carrying your baby, at the least, the very least, she deserves better than that from you. Propositioning her, like a whore, in front of mum and dad, is not cool. From what Tony told me, Cassidy turned and walked away, mum was in tears, and Tony just left you on the couch to sleep.

"You're right." What else could Jax say? His brother was right, not about everything, but about propositioning Cassidy. Jax was horrified that he had done that, no wonder Cassidy wasn't talking to him this morning, goodness only knows what she thought of him right now. He had to fix this, somehow, he had to make this right with her.

As Jax slid into his car and turned the engine over, he thought about last night. He knew what it must have looked like to his parents and to Cassidy, but he knew that wasn't what was happening, the only trouble was, would they believe him if he told them the truth? He wasn't so sure. Jax pulled in behind Kyle, the two of them walking inside together, finding everyone else back in the kitchen, tidying up.

"Mum, Tony, about last night...I'm sorry for acting like a fool, it wasn't what it seemed, and I'd like to explain everything later, but first, I need to talk to Cassidy."

"I have no interest in listening to anything you might have to say to me right now, Jax," Cassidy spoke from the doorway, "I'm ready to go if you are?" She addressed his mother and Jules.

"Where are you going?" Jax asked, thinking that he might go as well, and find some way of making last night up to her.

"Girl's day out," his mother answered. "Don't worry, we'll be home for dinner." And with that, his mum, Jules, and Cassidy swept out of the room, leaving him with Kyle, Tony, and his niece and nephew.

Annoyed with himself, and frustrated, Jax headed into the triple garage, part of which had been turned into a music studio of sorts for him over the years. Picking up an acoustic guitar, he flopped on the worn-out couch and started to strum, meaningless notes at first, until a riff started to form, and Jax grabbed some paper and a pen and jotted down the notes before he forgot them.

"I don't mind, I'll use the time, mmm-hmm mmm mm-hmm," he hummed, "cause I want to do things right, but I stuff up all the time," he added the words to his scrawled music notations, "I want to change my ways-"

121

"Good, you should," Kyle's voice broke through Jax's concentration, and he set his guitar to the side. "Sorry, I didn't mean to interrupt your songwriting."

"No, it's fine, I was just thinking things through."

"Okay, well, come up to the house, Tony has lunch ready."

"Really?" Tony wasn't known for cooking.

"Yep, he went all out," Kyle joked, "and ordered in pizza." Laughing, Jax joined his brother, pushing all thoughts of Cassidy from his mind.

CHAPTER FOURTEEN - CASSIDY

If Cassidy had thought that the sideways glances at dinner the night before last had been bad, the tense, guilty glances she was getting now as she, Judy, and Jules went around the larger shopping centre in Tamworth were utterly unbearable. Still, apart from the looks of pity, Cassidy was enjoying herself. She had never been on a girl's day out, but from what she could gather, it was essentially a combination of shopping, gossip, and lattes. Cassidy found the most divine baby clothes while in a boutique looking for something for Max's upcoming baptism, but as tempted as she was, she put them back down, not wanting to go against Jax's wishes and reveal their secret to his family just yet. As they were on their way to lunch, Cassidy excused herself to go to the bathroom, as far as side effects went, this one was far preferable to the constant, unrelenting morning sickness, that was for sure. As Cassidy sat down on the toilet, she saw something that literally made her heart stop. She was bleeding. No. No, no, no, she could not lose this baby, not now. The moment Cassidy had seen the blood, she had known that she wanted this baby, that she loved this baby, and would fight for this baby. What kind of cruel, cruel world was this? Cassidy was frozen in place, she couldn't breathe, tears clouded her vision, racing down her cheeks as sobs tore from her chest, shoulders shaking. She couldn't think straight. She finished in the bathroom and went straight out to the food hall, easily locating Jules and Judy, who jumped up, alarmed, at Cassidy's tears.

"I need to go to the hospital, now," Cassidy stuttered through her tears, "I'm pregnant and I'm bleeding," sobs tore at her chest as Judy gathered her into her arms.

"Oh, my darling, shh, it's okay, everything will be okay," the two women led Cassidy to the carpark and settled her into the car in silence, driving as fast as they dared to the local hospital. Cassidy watched as the scenery flashed by, blurry and uncertain, much like her life. As they drove through the streets towards the hospital, life went on around them. Kids played in the local park, people queued outside a fast-food restaurant, and cars honked at the lights, wanting to move. Cassidy saw none of this, her eyes unfocused, picturing the brown-haired baby she might never get the chance to know. It was a tense and quiet ride to the hospital.

"Cassidy," Judy broke the silence, "does Jax know about the baby?"

"Yes," Cassidy replied flatly, no longer caring about Jax or his wishes, "he's always known." Once they arrived at the hospital, Cassidy explained to the triage nurse what had happened, and she ushered Cassidy right through, leading her down through the emergency department to a special section dedicated to maternity and genealogical patients, asking Judy and Jules to wait outside, before drawing the curtains.

"Come on sweetie, let's get you up into bed, okay?" the nurse didn't wait for an answer, instead, she bustled about, turning down the sheets and helping Cassidy up onto the bed.

"I'm so cold," Cassidy's entire body was shaking.

"Shh, there you go sweetie, let's get you warmed up, hey?" Cassidy found herself enveloped in warmth as her nurse added two more heated blankets to her bed. A box of tissues appeared at her bedside table, and the nurse patted her hand gently.

"Please try not to worry sweetie, there are a number of reasons for bleeding during early pregnancy, and not all of them are negative or serious. It is important to try and stay calm for the baby, okay?" Cassidy nodded. "Would you like me to show your mum and sister in?" Cassidy nodded again, not bothering to correct her, as Judy and Jules rushed to her bedside.

"Cassidy, I called Jax, I hope that was okay?" Judy spoke softly.

"You shouldn't have bothered, Judy, he doesn't want me." Her voice sounded so small, even to her own ears, and she closed her eyes against the looks of compassion from the other women, too numb to care.

Time dragged on for Cassidy as her nurse came and went, drawing blood samples and checking her vital signs. Eventually, Cassidy heard the soft sound of male voices, her resolve hardening inside.

"Cassidy?" Jax's voice sounded close to her ear. In response, Cassidy rolled over until her back was facing him, no longer caring about being polite.

"Now that your husband is here, I'm going to have to insist that everyone else waits in the family waiting room down the hall, we have very strict visiting policies in cases like this, and Cassidy needs her rest." Her nurse added another blanket to her bed. "If you'll all follow me, I'll show you where you can all wait." Cassidy opened her eyes, at last, staring up at the white ceiling, glad that the room was empty apart from Jax, although she wished that he would leave her in peace as well. She was alone. Just her and Jax and a gulf of empty dreams and regrets between them. Cassidy wanted to correct the nurse, to scream that Jax wasn't hers nor had he ever been, to tell her that Jax meant nothing more to her than a one-night stand, but she couldn't, Cassidy knew the words were lies, and they had withered to dust on her sandpaper tongue before she could speak them.

"I can't lose this baby, it's all I have," Cassidy closed her eyes as sobs overtook her again.

"Cassidy," Jax's voice sounded croaky, cracked, strained with emotion. "Don't say that, you don't know anything for certain yet." Cassidy knew his words were meant to comfort her, but she was unable to stop the tears that fell. She cried Jax, for the man that she had fallen in love with, for the man that had never wanted her. She cried for her baby, for the longing she now felt for them, the love, for the adventures she would miss. Mostly, she cried for herself, for having been so cruelly denied a dream she had kept safely hidden for so long. Cassidy knew that no matter what, she would never again let anyone close to her, for any reason. She knew that this hurt was something that she would never recover from and never allow herself to risk feeling again.

"Hush Cassidy, the doctor will be here soon, they'll run some tests, we don't know anything for sure, okay, nothing is certain yet."

Cassidy closed her eyes again, imagining that the nurse had been right, that Jax was her husband. In the few minutes that they sat waiting for the doctor, Cassidy imagined it all. She saw her and Jax living together, sharing everyday things that couples share, she saw their children, growing up surrounded by their cousins and family that loved them. She saw large birthdays and celebrations, people being cherished and wanted, loved. With the doctor's arrival also came her bleak reality. Jax was not hers, she reminded herself sternly, he never was and he never would be. The doctor ran through a list of questions with Cassidy, checking her dates and recording her pregnancy symptoms and side effects, and once satisfied that they had the information they needed, told her that he would arrange for an ultrasound to be done first thing the following day, at which point he would be listening for a heartbeat. He would not discuss anything further with them now, preferring to do the ultrasound first.

"I'll just do a quick exam first, and then we'll arrange for an initial ultrasound, it won't be as detailed as the one I have scheduled you for tomorrow, but it's a start," the doctor spoke to them as he snapped on his gloves.

CHAPTER FIFTEEN - JAX

"I'll just do a quick exam first, and then we'll arrange for an initial ultrasound, it won't be as detailed as the one I have scheduled you for tomorrow, but it's a start," the doctor spoke to them as he snapped on his gloves. Once the exam was over, Jax entered the room and went to stand at the head of Cassidy's bed while the doctor and nurse prepared the portable ultrasound machine. Jax felt ill, physically and emotionally. This was all his fault. If he had never spoken to Cassidy in the supermarket, he would never have asked her for coffee, or to come with him to the festival, and they would never have hooked up, never have been intimate, and she would never have fallen pregnant. Not that he could regret the baby, he didn't, regardless of the circumstances of its conception. Only now....Jax shook his head. He should have taken Cassidy to the doctor days ago, he should never have gone to the barbecue and caused her all of that extra stress, stress which he was still causing her, he knew it. He still hadn't had a chance to apologise to her, to explain, and by the way she reacted when he walked in here, she was still, rightly so, angry with him. Once the ultrasound machine was set up, Cassidy lifted her dress up over her stomach and once the gel was squirted on, the doppler began to move around, grainy images appearing on the screen. Jax held his breath, although he had no idea why, he couldn't make out anything that was appearing on the screen.

"Okay, it's mixed news, I'm afraid," the doctor started, "your human chorionic gonadotropin hormone levels are still very high. This hormone is only made during pregnancy, almost exclusively in the placenta. Levels rise a lot during the first trimester and could explain why you have been suffering so badly with nausea and vomiting. The level would indicate that the pregnancy is still viable, but we will need to retest it in the coming days. Now, I couldn't detect a heartbeat, but," he looked at Cassidy, "that might not necessarily mean anything, it might simply be too early to hear it yet. I know this is hard, I know from personal experience how difficult this is for you, but I am going to send you home now and I want you to try and relax, try not to worry or get stressed. Tomorrow, hopefully, the tests will be more conclusive." Jax wasn't happy about taking Cassidy home, he felt it was better for her to stay in the hospital, what if something went wrong in the night? He excused himself to go and let his family know, telling them that they would be leaving in the next hour so there was no need for them all to stay any longer.

"When the two of you get home, Jax, and Cassidy is settled into bed, you and I are going to have a chat about just why exactly you decided to keep this news from us, and just what exactly you intend to do now, do I make myself clear?" His mother snarled at him. "No one deserves to go through what she went through today, I don't care if you love her or not, this is your responsibility, do you hear me?"

"Yes, Mum."

"Okay then, I'll see you at home." His mum and Tony left first, hugging him on the way out, followed by Jules and then Kyle, who fixed him with a sad look, shaking his head.

"Listen," he started once Jules had turned the corner with their parents, "don't be too hard on yourself, okay? I know what you are going through, we never said anything, but

Jules and I went through this when we were eighteen."

"What?" Jax was genuinely surprised, he and Kyle shared everything, to think that Kyle had kept this secret for a decade stunned Jax.

"We had just graduated, and neither of us was as careful as we should have been. I knew that I would marry her one day, but we hadn't made any firm plans, so when she found out she was pregnant, it was stressful. There was a lot of blame, and regret, but eventually, it started to seem like an adventure, you know? When she lost the baby, it nearly ruined us. We hadn't told anyone that she was pregnant, so there was no one there to help comfort her, apart from me, and I never knew the right thing to say. I was hurting too, but I tried to be tough for her, to keep her going. Eventually, we made it through, but that was why we never planned on more children, we weren't sure we were ready. That is also why we told everyone as early as we could, just in case something went wrong again, I know some people thought Jules was neurotic during her pregnancy, but she was just so scared, as was I, but we couldn't speak about it."

"I wish you'd told me; I could have listened if nothing else."

"I know, I'm sorry, but at the time, I was respecting Jules's wishes." The two brothers hugged goodbye, Jax returning to Cassidy's room to find her already dressed and ready to go.

"Where's your mum?" Cassidy frowned when he entered the room alone. "I thought you went to get everyone?"

"She and dad already left, I told them not to wait, that we'd be close behind them." Jax shrugged, holding out his hand to help Cassidy off the bed.

"I see," she said icily, ignoring his hand and hopping down herself.

"Cassidy, please, let me explain about last-"

"Don't talk to me," she stated, "I'm not interested in whatever you have to say, I just want to go home and go to bed." Once Jax had Cassidy buckled into the car, he tucked a blanket around her, and moved to the driver's seat, starting the engine and pulling out of the hospital carpark. He had sent his mum a text message before they had left, telling her what the doctor had said, and that they were on their way home, and he knew she would have something prepared to tempt Cassidy's appetite once they got home. He also knew that he would have more explaining to do, to his mum and to Cassidy, if only she would give him the chance. They drove in silence, Cassidy staring out of the window and Jax shooting worried glances at Cassidy.

Spotting a road sign, Jax pulled his car over into a road stop area and parked. Cassidy looked at him questioningly.

"The doctor said that gentle exercise every hour or so would help, let's get out and have a little walk around." Cassidy sighed but didn't argue, getting out of the car and wandering aimlessly in the direction of the walking trail. Jax ached to follow her but held himself back. He knew that she wouldn't welcome his company, she had already made that abundantly clear. He had no idea how he was going to fix this, how he could repair all of the stuff-ups that he had made with Cassidy. He knew she deserved so much better than him, but selfishly, he didn't want her to go.

CHAPTER SIXTEEN - CASSIDY

As much as Cassidy didn't want to be walking around, she had to admit, it did feel good to be moving. This rest stop had a path of sorts, that wove around the toilet block and through a small patch of parkland, the scent of eucalyptus and wattle on the air, and breathing every in helping relieve Cassidy's tension. She knew she shouldn't be so angry at Jax, he was being nothing but kind to her, but she couldn't help it. She was embarrassed to be stuck here with him when he so obviously wanted to be with another woman. She wondered if he had seen her today while she had been out shopping with his mother and sister-in-law. Cassidy sighed, looking glum, it didn't matter anymore now, did it? She had absolutely nothing to offer Jax, and nothing to hold him to her, at least with the baby she might have seen him from time to time, but now...She shook her head to dispel the depressive images of her sitting at home at the table, alone, while dust and grime piled up around her. As Cassidy rounded the corner of the path, she caught sight of Jax leaning against his car, legs crossed in front of him, arms crossed over his chest. His hair was moving slightly in the breeze and her breath caught in her throat, he really was the most handsome man she had ever met.

Even now, as tired and as devastated as she was, she still wanted him, she ached for him, she yearned to feel his hands on her skin, to have his lips pressed into hers once more. Just once more, was that so wrong to want, to crave? It had been weeks since he had touched her, but she still hungered for his touch, did that make her pathetic, to long for him so much? With a sob, she realised that it probably did. She couldn't help the way she felt, she just wanted what everyone else had, a partner, a life, happiness. Why was that so hard? Why was that too much for her to ask for, to hope for? Why did everything in life have to be so very hard for Cassidy, why did she always have to struggle so for every single thing that she ever had? Everyone around her seemed to get things so easily, it wasn't fair, what had she ever done to deserve such a rubbish life? After everything that she had to endure at the hands of her parents, she just wanted one thing to be easy, just one thing, why couldn't she have that?

Cassidy's steps stalled, she just wanted to stay here and watch Jax, to commit him to memory, before she lost him forever. With a heavy sigh and a broken heart, Cassidy returns to the car, watching Jax as she approached.

"Jax," she choked out, flinging herself against his chest, breathing in his scent as her tears soaked through his shirt.

"Cassidy," Jax's voice is thick with feeling, and without thinking about her actions, Cassidy tilts her head up, her lips pressing against his as Jax tangled his hands through her hair, tugging gently to tilt her head even further. Cassidy moaned softly as Jax deepened the kiss, desperate to have him closer still, her hands splayed out across his chest. Arching her back, Cassidy thrust her breasts towards Jax and hooked one of her legs around his, uncaring of just who could see them right now. Jax swung them around in a fluid movement, Cassidy's back anchored to his car, his hands trailing down her back to cup her soft bottom. Her breath ragged, Cassidy thrust her hips slightly until her core collided with Jax's erection, straining against the zip of his jeans, earning a hiss from Jax.

"Mm-hmmm, yes, Jax, Jax, Jax, Jax, Jax, oh, yes, please, please, I need…" Cassidy murmured feverishly, slipping her hands beneath the waistband of Jax's jeans to cup his erection. With a curse, Jax pushed her away harshly.

"Cassidy, stop it! That's enough!" Reality crashes down on Cassidy like a wave, a tsunami of regret and humiliation swirls around her, washing away all that she had left. Without a word, she slid back into her seat, closing her eyes and wrapping loneliness around her as a shield, blocking everything else out. She could sense Jax's eyes on her but refused to acknowledge him.

"We're home," he told her flatly a short while later. Home, she almost scoffed out loud, she didn't have a home, never had, not a real one in any case. She had a house that she slept in, but that was that, there was nothing else there that could have made it into a home, no love, no laughter, no family. It was an empty shell, like everything else in her life, like her very existence. As painful as the experience was for her, Cassidy allowed Judy and Jules to lead her through to the bedroom, change her into her nightie, and get her settled into bed, punishing

139

herself with their kindness, knowing that once she was back in Alice Springs, she would torture herself with these memories, these feelings, building up a series of what ifs to keep her awake at night. Cassidy never realised just how lonely she was until she met Jax, and now she saw it for what it was. It wasn't to protect her as she had often claimed, no, being alone was her own self-imposed prison, a lifetime of punishment for never being enough for anyone. Once Cassidy was tucked in, Judy and Jules left, and Jax came in, weighed down by bottled water and a tray of snacks, which he placed on the bedside table.

"Is there anything you need, anything I can get you?" He asked softly. Cassidy shook her head. When it was obvious that she wasn't going to say anything, he stood and made for the door.

"I'm sorry I kissed you," she blurted, stopping Jax in his wake, "back at the rest stop, I'm sorry, I know that was uncomfortable for you, I know that wasn't what you wanted." She released a sigh. "It won't happen again, I promise."

"Cassidy-" Jax turns back to face her.

"No, Jax, let me say this, okay? I know I am not your type, after the other night, I think we all know what your type is, don't we?" She shot him a wan smile. "It's okay, I don't expect you to say anything or to make excuses, we both know that I was never your type, never someone that you would ever choose, ever want," she bit out, "and that's fine, but no matter what happens tomorrow, I don't want you to stay. I don't need you to stay anymore," she lied. "I appreciate your gesture of support, I do, but it is for the best if this ends now, okay?" She took a deep breath. "So go, I'm letting you go, go and be with the skinny model-like girl who had you so hard the other night, Jax, go and be happy. I'll let you know if anything changes with the baby." She closed her eyes against the hurt look she saw on Jax's face, and rolled over, snuggling under the covers, until she heard him leave, closing the door behind him.

CHAPTER SEVENTEEN - JAX

"I'm sorry I kissed you," the words stopped Jax in his tracks. "Back at the rest stop, I'm sorry, I know that was uncomfortable for you, I know that wasn't what you wanted," Cassidy sighed. "It won't happen again, I promise."

"Cassidy-" Jax turned back to face her, to finally explain, to set her mind at ease.

"No, Jax, let me say this, okay? I know I am not your type, after the other night, I think we all know what your type is, don't we?" She shot him a wan smile. "It's okay, I don't expect you to say anything or to make excuses, we both know that I was never your type, never someone that you would ever choose, ever want," her words, spoken as truth, tore at Jax's heart, "and that's fine, but no matter what happens tomorrow, I don't want you to stay. I don't need you to stay anymore, I appreciate your gesture of support, I do, but it is for the best if this ends now, okay?" Jax couldn't breathe, what was she saying? "So go, I'm letting you go, go and be with the skinny model-like girl who had you so hard the other night, Jax, go and be happy. I'll let you know if anything changes with the baby." Jax stood there, stunned, staring at Cassidy as she closed her eyes and ignored him. When she still didn't move, he turned and left, finding himself yet again in the garage, guitar in hand.

This, right here, guitar in hand, was how Jax worked through everything, every problem he had ever had could be worked out, and had been worked out, with his guitar. He picked up the song he had started working on yesterday and added a few notations.

"I don't want to hear about the silence, I heard it once or twice, in another life," he sighed, why did he keep circling back to this? To silence, mistakes, and apologies not given. "But if you need to take some time, to fight those demons in your mind, well, I don't mind, I'll use the time because I love you, I love you, I love you, I hate you...I don't mind, I'll use the time, mmm-hmm mmm mm-hmm," he hummed, "cause I want to do things right, but I stuff up all the time," he sighed and stopped strumming. It was true, he did stuff up all the time, and all it did was hurt the people he loved. He shouldn't have walked away from Cassidy, he should have stayed and told her the truth,

143

made her listen to him. Why hadn't he? What had he been so afraid of?

He wished he had spoken to her, there were so many things, so many misunderstandings that he needed to, wanted to, tell her about. Now that it seemed like they had lost the baby, he wondered if she would ever give him the chance to talk to her again? It was unlikely, he realised, she seemed to have her mind already made up, not that he could blame her. So far, he hadn't given her much proof that he could be trusted, he had handled everything badly, like a scared teenager really, ever since he had started texting her while he was in Brisbane. He never should have done that, but once he had started, he knew that he should have ended it differently, kinder, like an adult. Urgh! Everything was so messed up! Even now, when he wants to be talking to her, he is in the garage instead, thinking about talking to her. He was...hurt, he decided, by the way she had simply ended things with him, which was pretty rich coming from Jax, who had never wanted a relationship in the first place. Not that that was what they had, far from it, but still, he was hurt, nonetheless. Maybe a bit put out that he hadn't ended things first, that she

144

had been the one to make that decision, which was petty, he knew.

As Jax sat in the garage wallowing in self-pity, his brother stopped in to tell him that he and Jules were heading home, and a short while later his mum interrupted him to let him know that she and Tony were ducking into town to pick up some dinner and to check that he would be okay here with Cassidy.

"Give me some credit, mum," Jax snapped, tired of everyone thinking that he was the villain here, even though he knew it was true. Knowing that he and Cassidy were alone in the house gave Jax pause. He should go and talk to her, now would be a perfect time. If she decided to yell at him, no one would be around to overhear it, nor would anyone be privy to what he wanted to tell her. A glint of something white had Jax looking up, a taxi was turning out of the driveway. Honestly, they always turned into Jax's parent's house, thinking it was the street they were looking for, the curse of living on a corner and having a long driveway he suspected. Deciding it was now or never, Jax rose and went inside, heading for the bedroom and Cassidy. He knocked quietly before walking into the bedroom he was currently sharing with Cassidy, not wanting to wake her if she was already sleeping. She wasn't in bed, which had been perfectly made, and a quick look in the ensuite showed it was also empty. With an uneasy feeling, Jax looked around the room for her suitcase, finding none, and a look in the wardrobe confirmed what he already knew. She was gone.

CHAPTER EIGHTEEN - CASSIDY

Cassidy looked around the hotel room and grimaced. She was a coward, she knew that, but once everyone had left the house and it was just her and Jax, she knew she had to act fast, tossing everything she could find of hers into the suitcase and calling a taxi. It was sheer luck that Jax hadn't come looking for her. She had taken a taxi straight back to Tamworth, it would easier that way, she could still get to the hospital tomorrow for her scan, and it would give her easy access to the airport, already having decided that she would not travel back to Alice Springs with Jax, but rather get a plane instead. She dumped the suitcase near the hotel room door, turned her mobile phone off, and, without bothering to undress, crawled into the large bed, where she cried herself to sleep. When Cassidy woke, she was bathed in light, having forgotten to close the curtains before hopping into bed, and it took her a moment to remember where she was, squinting out at the plush décor. With a groan, Cassidy sat up and stretched. Her throat was as dry as sandpaper, a quick look in the mini bar produced a small bottle of milk and after opening a few cupboards, Cassidy located a kettle, mugs and tea supplies. Once her tea was ready, Cassidy crawled back under the covers and switched on the television, watching a breakfast news program while she sipped the hot liquid.

Feeling better after her hot tea, Cassidy headed for the bathroom, she needed to be at the hospital soon for her follow-up ultrasound. As she undressed for the shower, there were no signs of any more bleeding, and, numb, Cassidy stepped into the shower, allowing the warm water to wash her tears away. She knew it was silly, her emotions were all over the place, it was just that while she was still bleeding, she was still, technically, pregnant, and now that it had stopped, she felt empty, bereft of all hope. That was it then, her brief stint at motherhood was over, and she hadn't even felt the baby move, would never feel her baby move. Cassidy felt so guilty, she hadn't even known that she had wanted her baby, not really, until it was too late, and now they would never know that they were wanted, her biggest fear had been realised, Cassidy thought as sobs overtook her,

her whole body shaking. She had failed as a mother, before she had even really begun, she had failed, her child hadn't known that they were wanted. It was a long time until Cassidy's sobs subsided, and she was finally able to dress and head to the hospital, resigned to her fate.

The hospital radiology unit was cold, the waiting room already full, with a variety of injuries on display. Cassidy found a seat between a man in a leg cast and a woman in an arm cast and waited. It wasn't long until she heard her name being called and she stood and followed the radiology technician through to an exam room where an ultrasound machine was already set up. After getting as comfortable as was possible on the hospital bed, Cassidy answered the same questions that she had had to answer yesterday, confirming her dates, listing her symptoms, and discussing her bleed, before, finally, the technician asked her to lift her shirt up and squirted the cold gel onto her stomach. The sonographer turned the screen away from Cassidy, who was relieved at the thoughtful gesture and touched the doppler onto her stomach, starting the scan. Cassidy laid there in the silence, willing herself not to look at the sonographer's face, not wanting to see her expression, not wanting to read anything into it. The only sounds Cassidy could hear were the whooshing of her blood vessels and the beating of her heart.

"I'm sorry it has taken so long, Cassidy," the radiographer spoke, turning to her with a gentle smile, "but I wanted to confirm my results before I spoke to you." Cassidy nodded, already knowing what the radiographer was going to say. "Is there anyone with you today, in the waiting room maybe, that you'd like me to call in with you?"

"No, thank you, please, just tell me."

"Okay, Cassidy," the radiographer nodded. "I know that you presented in the emergency department yesterday with bleeding, or spotting, and there was some concern that they couldn't hear your baby's heartbeat. I wish they'd called me immediately, instead of making you wait all night because I can tell you right now that your baby has a strong heartbeat."

"What?" Cassidy was confused.

"You didn't lose the baby, Cassidy, the baby is strong and healthy, and looking at your scan your dates are spot on."

"I...what?" Cassidy burst into tears, embarrassed and happy. She hadn't lost her baby, Jax's baby, she was still pregnant. She couldn't think straight, didn't know what to feel, she had another chance, another chance at being a good mum. "I...I don't understand, how?" The radiographer passed Cassidy a box of tissues and smiled down at her.

"There is any number of reasons why they couldn't hear a heartbeat, it might simply have been too quiet, too early, maybe the baby was in the wrong spot...That isn't all, Cassidy," the radiographer turned the screen around for Cassidy to see, "this," she pointed to an image on the screen, "is your baby, and this," she pointed to another image on the screen, "is your second baby. You're expecting twins."

"Two?" Cassidy couldn't believe it, there were two babies in there?!

"Two," the radiographer confirmed with a chuckle. "It is a bit of a shock isn't it, your poor thing, you must have had a horrid night." Cassidy merely nodded in reply. "Bleeding isn't uncommon in early pregnancy, especially more with twins. It could also explain your horrid morning sickness. Do twins run in your family?"

"No," Cassidy shook her head, still in a daze.

"I know you're only visiting here, but if you have any more concerns while you are here, don't hesitate to come back, okay? Meanwhile, you might like to reach out to your multiple birth organisation in your own state, they are a great resource, and you will have the opportunity to meet other parents of multiples who can be a great support." The sonographer printed out a series of photos of the babies and handed them to Cassidy who stashed them safely in her handbag before leaving.

Cassidy returned to the waiting room in a daze, still not quite believing what had just happened. She would have to tell Jax, again. She wondered how he would react to the news of there being twins? As she approached the reception to check out, she stopped dead in her tracks, there at the reception desk stood Judy and Jax. Cassidy briefly thought about avoiding them, of just leaving, but decided against it, that would be petty and mean, and she was neither of those things.

"Judy," Cassidy spoke softly, Judy whipping around to see her, relief on her face.

"Cassidy, oh, thank goodness!" Judy rushed to embrace her, Cassidy hugging the older woman back, ignoring Jax's gaze. "We were worried sick!"

"Oh, I'm sorry, I didn't think it would matter that much."

"You didn't think it would...Oh my dear girl," Judy shook her head, "of course it matters to us, you matter to us, now, let's get you checked out and go somewhere quiet to talk, hmm?" Cassidy merely nodded and went along with Judy's plans, still too overwhelmed to think straight. Once Cassidy had checked out, Judy asked her where she was staying, and they all drove back to the hotel together, nobody speaking until they were safely inside Cassidy's hotel room and seated comfortably.

"Cassidy, can you forgive me?"

"You?" Cassidy was confused. "Whatever for?"

"I had wanted to come alone today, to your appointment, in the hopes of seeing you, of talking to you, but Jax insisted on coming as well. I realise that you don't want to see him, I apologise if I overstepped the boundary today by bringing him with me."

"Oh." Cassidy frowned. Is that really what they all thought? That she didn't want to see Jax? "No, that's fine, I didn't leave because I didn't want to see Jax, I left so that he could be happy," Cassidy smiled wryly. "Jax never told you that I was pregnant, I think subconsciously, he was hoping that it wasn't viable."

"No!" Jax blurted out. "That isn't it at all, Cassidy, I didn't tell you," he turned to face his mother, "because it would have meant too many questions about Cassidy and me, questions that I wasn't ready to answer."

"What he means Judy, is that Jax and I were never in a relationship. It was simply a one-night stand, that's all. Jax owes me nothing, he did more than most men would have, and we reached an agreement of sorts. We'll move in together, as flatmates, and co-parent the baby, that plan has obviously changed now."

"I'm so sorry, sweetie, do you want to tell us what the sonographer said?" Judy asked, her voice and her eyes full of compassion for Cassidy.

"Well, I'm not sure where to start," Cassidy chewed her bottom lip. "Firstly, it turns out that I am, in fact, still pregnant. The heartbeat is nice and strong and my dates are correct."

"Oh," Judy clapped her hands together, "that is wonderful news!"

154

"Also, "Cassidy continued, watching Jax's face carefully, "I'm expecting twins."

"Twins," Jax echoed, a slow smile spreading across his face. "Cassidy, we're having twins? That's fantastic!"

"Twins," Judy sniffed, tears sliding down her cheeks, "I'm going to double my grandbabies in one swoop," she smiled a dreamy smile. "Oh, my goodness!" Judy suddenly exclaimed. "There is so much to do, I'll need to buy another cot, and two more car seats, and some more clothes, oh," she paused, unexpectedly, looking at Cassidy shyly, "I mean, that is if you will let us be a part of their lives?" Cassidy was shocked that Judy would even have to ask, but then again, she realised that she knew very little about family dynamics.

"Judy, no matter what happens with Jax and me, you will always be a part of the babies' lives."

CHAPTER NINETEEN - JAX

With a squeal, his mother jumped up and wrapped Cassidy in another of her vice-like hugs. Twins. Jax couldn't believe it, only a couple of months ago he was single and carefree, and now he was the father of twins. Jax felt slightly ill at the prospect of having the responsibility for two children, and the very real possibility that he would let everyone down. As he sat and listened to his mother waffle on about her shopping plans, he noticed that Cassidy looked tired.

"Mum," he interrupted, "maybe we should let Cassidy rest? She's had an exhausting few days."

"Of course. Will you come back home and stay with us, Cassidy?"

"If you would like me to, I'll stay for the weekend. I have a flight booked for Monday." Jax tried not to feel disappointed at the news that she had already arranged an alternative way back to Alice Springs, he should have expected it, after the way he had acted, he was surprised that she had stayed as long as she had.

"Well, then," his mother beamed, "we'll go and let you rest. Maybe we'll go do some shopping, Jax," Jax tried not to let his horror show, "and we'll come back in a few hours to pick you up. If you wake up before then, just shoot Jax a text message, Cassidy, and we'll come straight away."

In the end, Jax and his mother went to the local shopping mall, Jax to find a music store, and his mother to find a baby store, Jax warning her not to go overboard. He knew that Cassidy would not appreciate it, she was not used to being taken care of, or being cared for, or being spoilt. His mother would need to go slow with Cassidy if she wanted to have a close relationship with her, as she did with Jules. Patting his forearm, she assured him that she knew that, and strode off. His mother found him in the music store a short while later, having already finished the shopping that she had wanted to do. As there was no message from Cassidy yet, Jax offered to drive his mother home, and return straightaway for Cassidy, wanting a few minutes alone with her before she returned home with him. Cassidy texted Jax just as he was pulling into a parking spot at the hotel, and he went straight up to her room, only waiting for half a beat for the door to be wrenched open.

"Jax? Where's your mum?" Cassidy peered into the corridor behind him, frowning when she saw that it was empty.

"I dropped her home," he explained, "may I come in, please?"

"Sure," Cassidy stood aside to let him enter.

"Cassidy, I was hoping that we might talk for a few minutes before I take you home? I would like a chance to explain a few things to you if you are ready to listen to me?" Jax seated himself on the small armchair, leaving the bed for Cassidy.

"Jax, I-" Cassidy was going to refuse him, Jax just knew it.

"Please, Cassidy, it's important," he interrupted her, pressing.

"Okay," Cassidy finally answered, climbing up onto the bed and settling herself against the headboard, turning slightly to face Jax.

"Thank you," Jax started. "When I got to the barbecue and saw that Tara was there, I was furious, she and I have a history, and it isn't a particularly good one." Jax watched Cassidy carefully as he explained what Tara had done to his mum.

"Why then-" Cassidy stopped herself short, blushing.

"Why then would I want to go there again?" Jax supplied, quirking an eyebrow.

"Exactly."

"I wouldn't, Cassidy. We had all had a little too much to drink to be safe drivers, Tara was the only one who was sober. She was taking a carload of guests home, myself included."

"Okay." Cassidy sounded as if she didn't quite believe him.

"I was struggling to open the car door, so Tara got out to help, sarcastically asking if I needed help to get to the door. Unfortunately, I did. When we got halfway up the path, I tripped on the edge of mum's flower bed and fell, pulling her down with me. She was irked that I had ruined her evening, apparently, she had gone to the barbecue hoping I would rekindle things with her, which was never going to happen. Although, ah, she did say that, ah, her on top, straddling me, was certainly an improvement on her evening," Jax said, wanting to be honest with Cassidy, whatever the outcome.

"I'll bet she did," Cassidy muttered, just loud enough for Jax to hear her.

"I wasn't turned on by her Cass, it was you, standing there in the doorway, surrounded by a halo of light like my own personal angel," Jax admitted. "You were the reason I was hard, not her."

"Oh," Cassidy blushed furiously, "you were such a jerk about it."

"I was, I'm so sorry, Cass, I shouldn't have said that, especially not in front of others, I'm sorry if that made you feel uncomfortable."

"I don't want to not believe you, Jax," Cassidy stated, "but I need to know, are you telling me the truth now?"

"Yes," Jax didn't hesitate to answer.

"So then, why were you so mean to me when I tried to kiss you yesterday?" Cassidy stared straight at him as she spoke. "Especially, if, as you claim, you were so attracted to me the other night? I just don't understand."

"I'm so sorry, Cassidy, I know that hurt your feelings," Jax sighed. "I wanted you so much, believe me, if you had been well and we had been at home, I wouldn't have even paused to consider the ramifications, I would have just had you wrapped around me, screaming my

160

name. I didn't want to have to push you away Cassidy, I hope you know that. I was just so worried about you, about hurting you, about you confusing your feelings of loss for lust, of using you."

"Using me?"

"You put on a strong face, Cassidy, but I knew you were in pain. I didn't want to take advantage of you, comfort you, yes, but take advantage of you, no. I didn't want you to regret anything the following day."

"Thank you, Jax. I think you're right, I would have felt worse the following day. You're actually kind of sweet, aren't you?" At this, Jax laughed.

"I guess so, when the mood takes me. So, are we okay, Cassidy?"

"We will be, Jax, it just might take some time for us to find our groove."

"Where to from here? You know I am attracted to you, and I think that maybe, just maybe, you are attracted to me as well?" Jax prompted.

"Seriously, Jax? I think you're as hot as hades, I also think your heart and mind are pretty epic as well," she smiled at him, "but I don't think we should be physical, not now. I think we both need time to get used to our new reality and to adapt to the twins, get to know each other, properly, before we even think about anything else."

"I agree," Jax nodded, "as much as I want you, I want our friendship and the twins to come first, that is my priority, I don't want to stuff it up again."

"So, we have a truce?" Cassidy asked.

"We have a truce," Jax confirmed.

"Good. Oh, Jax, you can, you know, kiss me sometimes, if you want," Cassidy stuttered out.

"As you wish." With a grin, Jax stood and crossed to Cassidy, cupping her face gently in both of his hands and bringing his mouth down to hers, his tongue softly parting her lips, entering her mouth with confidence. His fingers tangled in her hair, and he angled her face, his tongue delving deeper inside, tasting every inch he could. With a groan, he tore himself away before they went too far, looking sheepishly down at Cassidy, who was just as affected by the kiss as he was. "Come on, let's get you checked out and back home before mum starts to worry." They walked downstairs hand in hand, Jax carrying Cassidy's suitcase. This was nice, he thought, just being with

Cassidy, sharing, having no secrets anymore. If he wasn't careful, Jax knew he could get used to this.

CHAPTER TWENTY - CASSIDY

The next couple of days pass in a blissful blur. Cassidy spends a good portion of each day napping, much to her embarrassment and Jax's amusement. Their relationship has shifted, no longer uncomfortable or awkward, their truce is easy, and Cassidy finds herself looking forward to the future. It's a nice change, having someone fuss over her, and she knows that she will miss it once she returns to Alice Springs and Jax returns to Brisbane. Cassidy wonders if their newfound relationship will last the separation and distance, but puts her worries to the side, not wanting to spoil the time that they do have together. Cassidy had become quite fond of Judy and was sorry that she lived so far away, it would have been nice to have a female around to talk to while she was pregnant, and said as much to Jax one afternoon.

"I'm sorry you don't have that with your own mother, Cassidy."

"As far as I'm concerned, I don't have a mother," she answered matter of fact.

"I know, and I'm still sorry. I can't imagine all of the things that you missed out on," he reached across and squeezed her hand. "You could call her you know, she'd love that." Cassidy thought that maybe she would take him up on that offer.

It was the day before Cassidy was due to fly back to Alice Springs, and she and Jax were laying on their bed, side by side, looking at the ultrasound photos that Cassidy had been given. She had already given one of them to Judy and Tony, who had promptly gone out and bought a frame to house it, adding it to their kitchen countertop so that they could see it every day. Cassidy thought it was a very sweet gesture, and it had made her cry. Mind you, just about everything made her tear up at the moment, silly hormones.

"What do you think they are?" Jax asked, peering at the photo. "Boys or girls?"

"I don't know," Cassidy shrugged, "maybe one of each? I forgot to ask what their genders were."

"Do you want to know?"

"I don't know, maybe, it would be nice to buy cute outfits for them, instead of all generic items, but then again, I suppose with two babies they will go through so many clothes we'll hardly notice what they are wearing. Do you want to know?" She asked curiously.

"I think we should wait."

"In that case, we'd better choose two names for boys and girls, just in case," Cassidy smiled over at Jax.

The following morning's breakfast was a noisy affair, the whole family gathering for Cassidy's last meal with them before heading back to Alice Springs, all of them needing to give her and the babies one more hug before she got in the car to leave. Cassidy was flattered, and unused to, such attention. She was glad that Jax had such a large, happy, loving family. That's what she wanted to give her babies, she decided, a family like that, and she would, Jax's family making it clear that they would be there for the babies, no matter what, which was nice of them. Jax drove her to the airport himself, he would leave for Brisbane from there, the drive into Tamworth a noisy affair, both Cassidy and Jax chatting non-stop. Cassidy kept thinking of something that she wanted to ask, or something that she wanted to know. They had agreed that once she was back in Alice Springs, Cassidy would go to the doctor and set up regular appointments, and she would reach out to the local multiple birth group. If Jax was unable to be with her for appointments, she would video conference him in, so that he didn't miss out on anything.

"Now, you have everyone's mobile numbers programmed into your mobile phone?" Jax asked for the millionth time.

"Yes, Jax, please don't worry."

"I can't help it, I want to make sure you know how to contact one of us if you need to."

"It's all under control, your mum has already said that she will call me every day as well, plus I expect you to call me," Cassidy teased.

"I'll call you every chance I get, Cassidy, you have my word," Jax replied, solemnly.

"Jax," Cassidy touched his arm lightly, "I was only joking, I know you will."

"Sorry," Jax apologised, "it's just that I want to do things right, you know? I don't want to stuff this up again."

"Jax," Cassidy looked into his face, "I'm pretty sure we'll both stuff up along the way, but as long as we're breathing, it is fixable, please don't be too hard on yourself."

They easily found parking at Tamworth Airport, and Jax carried her suitcase through to the check-in desk, making sure she was checked in and had the seat she wanted, before the two of them went and sat near the large windows overlooking the runways. While they waited for Cassidy's flight to be called, they enjoyed some plane watching, and a spot of people watching, both of them fascinated by the array of people coming and going. Eventually, her flight was called, and Cassidy stood slowly, looking at Jax.

"Will you call me once you are home safely?" He asked.

"I will," she promised him.

"Goodbye Cass," he pulled her close, holding her tightly, his mouth coming down to meet hers. His tongue slid over her lips, his teeth nipping at the plump mounds gently, before his tongue probed her lips, seeking entrance and which she gladly gave, melting into him with a sigh. As their tongues joined, dancing together, Jax deepened the kiss, and Cassidy tilted her head slightly, wanting him deeper still. Cassidy wound her arms up around Jax's neck, ruffling his hair with her fingers, loving the way he felt beneath her hands.

While one of Jax's hands rested on the small of her back, holding her close to him, the other one snaked its way down to rest gently on her stomach. It was Cassidy who broke the kiss, albeit reluctantly, and stepped away with a goofy grin on her face.

"Drive safely, Jax, please, for me, for us," she asked.

"I will." With one last kiss on his cheek, Cassidy turned and filed through departures, bound for Alice Springs.

CHAPTER TWENTY-ONE - JAX

"It was...painful," Cassidy sighed, "I think they might be starting to suspect something."

"Aww, honey, I'm sorry, I know that must have been hard on you," Jax soothed. "What do you want to do? Do you want to give up work?"

"I'd love to," Cassidy sighed again, "but there is no way that I can afford to do that, not with a mortgage."

"Cassidy, we've never really discussed this, have we? I can come back to Alice Springs, we can move in together, you can quit your job and let me take care of you, all of you," Jax offered.

"As nice of a thought as that is Jax, you know you can't do that. You have a contract, a commitment, to teach in Brisbane for this year, I don't want you to break that."

"My contract is up at the end of September, it was renegotiated yesterday, I have been waiting to talk to you, to tell you," Jax happily informed Cassidy. "I'll be back in Alice Springs, taking care of you, in a few weeks."

"Jax, that's wonderful!" Cassidy sounded close to tears.

"Cass?" Jax frowned.

"Sorry," she muttered, "hormones, it is so tiring, growing two humans." Jax could only imagine how hard Cassidy was finding it while she was essentially on her own.

"Tomorrow, when you go to work, hand in your resignation, effective the third week in September, that's only another month away, the time will fly. Or, better yet, put in for maternity leave, and then take leave without pay until the babies are born, I'm sure your doctor would issue you with a medical certificate, effective immediately, especially considering you are having twins. Then you can relax and put your feet up while I cater to your every wish and whim."

"Really? My every wish and whim?" Cassidy teased him, and an image of Cassidy laying naked with her legs splayed out, completely open for him on his bed, her core dripping wet and waiting for him, jumped unheeded into his mind, forcing Jax to bite down on a groan which Cassidy didn't miss.

"Jax? What are you doing?"

"Thinking about you naked, for me."

"Huh. Are you hard?" Jax could hear the smile in her voice.

"Yes," he admitted.

"You're so huge, Jax, big and thick," Cassidy purred, "I bet it hurts, doesn't it, straining against the fabric of your pants."

"Cassidy," Jax warned.

"Take your jeans off, Jax, now," Cassidy ordered, "let me help you." After a brief hesitation, Jax unzipped his jeans, sliding them down his legs and kicking them off. "And your boxer briefs," Cassidy added. "Are you naked, Jax?"

"Yes," he moaned, "I'm naked."

"Good, is anyone else home?"

"No." Which was a relief, Jax knew that when he came, he would come hard.

"Put me on speakerphone and get comfortable." Jax hurried to obey, his shaft throbbing painfully with every one of Cassidy's demands.

"Done." He had placed his phone on the bedside table and had sprawled out across his bed diagonally.

"Touch the tip of your cock for me, Jax, tell me what you feel."

"Beads of pre-cum," Jax gasped out, his breath ragged.

"Rub it all over your shaft, I want you to pretend that it is me, that it is my juices covering your cock, are you doing that Jax?"

"Yes."

"You're so big, did I ever tell you that? So thick and long, so thick, I love the way you stretch me, every time, Jax, my body stretches to fit you all in," Cassidy crooned. "Are you covered in your juices now, Jax?"

"Yes, Cass-"

"Grip on tight, as tight as you can, pretend that it is me, that you are buried inside me, my tight walls gripping you, my tight walls anchoring you to me, milking you, are you doing that, Jax, are you imaging that I'm there, bent over your desk, that you are plunging in and out of me?"

"Yes, Cass, yes," Jax grunted as he pumped his hand up and down his cock, faster and faster, gripping on as if his life depended upon it, the vision of Cassidy bent over his desk as he plunged into her from behind mesmerising.

"Faster, Jax, harder," Cassidy shouted, "deeper, deeper, oh, yes, just there baby, just there. Ooh, I love the way your balls slap against my thighs Jax, I love how deep you go inside me, so deep, so deep. Yes, you're so close now, so close, urgh, you're so big, Jax, so hard.

Oh, stab your throbbing cock into me, Jax, again, harder, harder, I want you to come for me, scream my name," Cassidy demanded.

"Cassidy, so close, so close," Jax muttered, not sure if he was being coherent or not at this point.

"Ooh, Jax, do you see my breasts, so big and round and just for you to play with, just you, Jax, my whole body is just for you. Come for me, Jax, claim me, make me yours, come inside me, deeper, deeper, Jax, Jax."

"Urgh, Cass, yes, yes, Cass, Cass, yes, yes, yes!" It was the calling of his name that was Jax's undoing, and with a scream of triumph, he emptied his load into his hand and across his bed, pumping frantically until every last drop had been expelled from his aching shaft, before collapsing, utterly spent, back on his pillows.

"Jax?" Cassidy's soft voice floated over to him. "Are you okay?" He could picture her, sitting there, chewing her bottom lip, a look of concern etched across her face.

"Cassidy, thank you, that was phenomenal," he declared. It was the first time that he and Cassidy had engaged in phone sex, the first time that he had engaged in phone sex at all, and he hoped it wouldn't be their last time. "I wish you were here so that I could show you exactly how good that was, so that I could make you feel that good, so that I could see you, watch your face, as you come undone for me."

"I miss you, Jax," Cassidy whispered.

"Cassidy, I miss you too, and I'm not just talking about being able to kiss you, to touch you, although I do, of course, miss that side of things immensely. I miss being close to you, holding your hand, seeing you smile, hearing your laugh. I wish we didn't live so very far away from each other; I wish I could watch as your body grows and changes, I know we video call each other, but I want to see the changes every day, I want to be able to touch your stomach as it grows round with my babies, I just want to be close to you."

"That's what I want too, Jax, more than anything. As you said, it is only another month and then you'll be back in Alice Springs."

"Would you come to Bingara with me? Once I finish up here, we could meet in Bingara for a week or so, and then drive back to Alice Springs together, a mini holiday of sorts, before our babies arrive." Jax had often referred to them as their babies, he liked the way that it sounded.

"I think I'd like that, Jax. Plus, it will give your family a chance to see us again before our babies get here, I don't suppose we'll travel much once they are born, not at first anyway."

They spent the rest of the call finalising their plans, plotting where they would stay and what they would do during their mini-break, before finally ending the call. Jax stayed lying in bed for a while longer, his hand absently trailing up and down his shaft, until he felt himself grow hard again, and he gripped himself firmly, picturing Cassidy's full breasts swaying from side to side, imaging her straddling him, sinking down onto his hard cock as she impaled herself on top of him, before moving, slowly at first, until lust and need overtook her senses and she began to move with wild abandon. Jax's hand moved up and down his aching cock, faster and faster, as visions of Cassidy riding him, coming undone around him while his cock thrust deeper and deeper inside of her, swam in his head. With a final grunt, Jax exploded, his cock spilling his juices all over his hand and onto the sheets. Once he could move again, Jax stood and stripped his bed, throwing his sheets into the wash and heading through to the shower, his thoughts on Cassidy. Not long now and he would have her in his arms again. If today's display was anything to go by, she was obviously missing him as much as he was missing her. He couldn't wait to get reacquainted.

The weeks flew by and before Jax knew it he was on his way from Brisbane to Tamworth. He and Cassidy had decided that he would pick her up first, and then together they would go to his parent's house. He had told his parents that he would be arriving sometime this weekend, but not exactly when, and he didn't mention that Cass would be joining him, the two of them deciding to surprise his family. He glanced at his watch for the umpteenth time. The arrivals board was still showing Cassidy's plane as arriving on time, yet there was still no sign of her. He crossed to the windows to watch the planes landing and taking off, an announcement finally being made about a delay, Cassidy's plane, by an hour. Jax took a seat on the hard plastic chairs and leaned back, waiting. He was the first one up and waiting when Cassidy's plane finally landed, a bit too eager maybe, as he then had to stand there, fidgeting, while passengers trickled off. When he finally saw Cassidy he strode over and swept her up into his arms, spinning her around and kissing her thoroughly, much to the amusement of those watching. When he finally let her go, he dropped to his knees and rested his face against her stomach, kissing his babies hello.

Jax could stay like this forever, with Cassidy safe in his arms. It felt right, it felt like home, he admitted to himself as he took her hand in his and they walked down to collect her luggage.

"Are you hungry?" Jax asked as his eyes ate her up. She looked tired, he would make sure she rested while she was here, no more stress or work would help as well.

"Yes," she giggled, "honestly, I feel like I haven't stopped eating in weeks." He was glad, and he knew that Cassidy was as well, her earlier morning sickness well and truly gone, to be replaced with an insatiable hunger and insomnia.

"Lunch it is," Jax smiled at her, stowing her suitcase in the boot of the car. Once they were buckled in, he drove them to the hotel that Cassidy had stayed in the last time she was in

Tamworth and parked, helping her out of the car without comment. He checked them into their room and led her over to the elevators.

"No questions, Cass?" Jax was surprised that she hadn't asked what they were doing here.

"I trust you," she replied simply. It was this trust that had him turning to her to cup her face, bringing his lips down to meet hers in a kiss full of longing and need.

As the elevator doors pinged open, Jax broke the kiss and stepped out, tugging Cassidy flush against his side as they made their way down the corridor to the hotel room. Once they were inside, Jax turned to her.

"Lunch?" He quirked an eyebrow at her, sliding the room service menu off the television unit.

"Jax," Cassidy's voice was full of longing, "make love to me?" She stepped closer to him. "Please?"

"Cass, are you sure?" He needed to hear that she was certain, that she wasn't just doing this because he wanted her. They had made an agreement, and he wasn't going to break it unless she was absolutely sure.

"I'm sure, Jax," Cassidy leaned up and kissed him along his jawline, "I want this," she slid her

179

hands down his torso, "I want you," she cupped his erection through the fabric of his pants. "I want you buried inside me, Jax, I need you buried inside me."

With a low groan, Jax swept Cassidy up into his arms and carried her through to the bedroom, setting her down carefully at the foot of the bed. Stepping back, Jax held Cassidy's gaze as he undressed, slowly discarding his boots and shirt, watching her eyes darken as she watched him. He released his fly slowly, shrugging out of his jeans and kicking them to the side, his boxer briefs following right behind. Smiling, Jax stepped up to Cassidy, capturing her mouth with his own, his teeth biting and nipping, sucking her bottom lip. He gripped the fabric of her dress, bunching it up in his hands and sliding it up over her buttocks, a delighted gasp escaping as his hands touched bare skin.

"No panties?" He asked, incredulous.

"G string," she panted, "although had I known..." she trailed off, Jax groaning at the thought. He would never have lasted all the way to the hotel had he known. He cupped her buttocks, lifting one of her legs up to hook around his waist, sliding his hand across the fabric of her panties at the apex of her thighs, feeling the wetness already soaking through the fabric.

He rubbed his finger back and forth a couple of times, marvelling at her wetness, loving the knowledge that it was he who had her dripping wet, her core pulsing with desire. Leaving his hand cupping her wetness, Jax dragged his mouth down to her breast, latching onto it through the fabric of her dress and suckling. With reluctance, Jax moved, lifting Cassidy's dress over her head and making quick work of her bra before returning his mouth to her breast, savouring the feel of her larger form. Jax suckled her nipple, flicking it with his tongue and nipping at it with his teeth as it pebbled beneath him, the hardened nub more sensitive than usual, loving the way Cassidy moaned and arched against him. With his erection throbbing, jutting out proudly for all to see, Jax lifted Cassidy and placed her on the bed, the sight of her flushed with need, her lips swollen, her legs splayed out, open and waiting for him was nearly his undoing and he joined her on the bed, lifting her legs over his shoulders and plunging into her dripping core without preamble, Cassidy shouting out as his hardened length drilled into her. She was so tight, always so tight, and he loved the feel of her as she stretched to fit him in, it was the hottest thing, being almost too big for her, his length and girth stretching and filling her completely.

Cassidy clung to him as he moved inside of her, deeper and deeper, until he was fully sheathed inside her, his balls resting at the bottom of her seam. She clung to his shoulders as he moved, pounding into her again and again, pulling out fully each time, before stabbing back into her core, relishing the feel of her stretching, of almost breaking under his size. He moved as in a fog, her screams and groans his guide, her wish his command. His speed increased, faster and faster until he worried he might send them through the bed, so frantic was their lovemaking. Cassidy ran her nails up and down Jax's back, before slipping a hand between them to grip one of his balls, squeezing it gently in her hand, shouting out as Jax stabbed into her deeper still. He could feel his length growing longer as he stabbed into her shaking core, again and again, he knew she was close. Reaching his hand between them both he found her bundle of nerves and gave it a sharp twist, sending her over the edge, joining her as her walls clamped down on his hard cock, milking him dry, her rolling spasms anchoring him inside of her, their mutual shouts of triumph filling the air around them.

Jax didn't want to leave her, he didn't want to pull out, he was enjoying her warmth too much, he loved how they fitted together so perfectly, he loved how she felt wrapped around his cock. As they lay there together in their post-lovemaking haze, Cassidy trailed her fingers up and down his arms, feathering kisses across his chest. Jax shifted slightly and sighed contentedly, his cock was already growing hard again inside of Cassidy, and he slid his hand down her side, adding one of his fingers inside of her core to join his cock, earning a hiss of delight from Cassidy. Hmm, he would have to try that more often. He slipped his finger out and slid it lower still, to circle and tease her puckered hole, slipping the tip in slightly, gauging Cassidy's reaction. By the sounds she was making, it looked like he could add that to their list of things to explore together. Lifting one of her knees up, Cassidy gave a push, rolling them both over with Jax still buried deep inside of her. She smiled down at him as she took his other hand and moved it to her sensitive nub, moaning loudly as he took the hint and began to swirl and roll it between his thumb and forefinger, pulling it lightly, then pinching it with a sharp twist. One thing he loved about Cassidy, she wasn't afraid to show him what she liked in bed, it was a huge turn-on, to have a sexually curious and vocal partner.

Jax watched, mesmerised, as Cassidy's breasts swayed and danced for him over her swollen stomach as she rode him slowly, rising up and then sinking down onto his length, a groan of pleasure leaving her lips each time. Tucking her feet behind her, Cassidy tilted her whole body back slightly, arching her back so that Jax could see his hard cock sliding in and out of her dripping core. Never before had he been granted such an uninterrupted view as he entered someone, and watching his cock disappear fully into Cassidy, seeing it slide out covered in her juices before disappearing again, watching as his balls slapped against the entrance to her centre, was quite literally the hottest thing he had ever seen, and he nearly came right then and there, a deep hiss leaving his lips. With a smile Cassidy leant down to touch his balls, shouting out as Jax bucked involuntarily beneath her, plunging even deeper into her dripping centre. Jax reached up and grabbed her hips, tethering her to his cock, his erection buried fully in her tight centre as Jax bucked and ground into her from below, Cassidy lifting her hips and meeting him thrust for thrust. He was so close, so close. Sliding his hands underneath her buttocks, he positioned one of his fingers at her puckered hole, just close enough so that she would bounce on it as she rode him, but not close enough to fully enter her, just enough to give her the added pleasure. With his other hand free, he slid a finger into her dripping core in time with his thrusting cock, delighting in the way she stretched even further, the surprise and shock on her face at the added sensations.

With his bulging cock and his finger both thrusting into Cassidy, Jax reached his thumb up and ran it across her bundle of nerves, tipping her over the edge with a wild scream, her walls clamping down on his swollen cock with such force it triggered his own release, his need filling her up and spilling over, their juices mingling on their skin. Jax knew that he would

185

never ever tire of watching Cassidy orgasm, she came so hard, it was refreshing to see her let everything go, she held nothing back, not even concerned with who might hear her. Hours later, both completely spent, Jax held her as she slept, curled into his side, completely naked, body entwined with his. Jax revelled in this feeling of rightness, of everything being as it should be in his world. He knew he had grown to love Cassidy, not that he had told her yet, but he had no intention of ever letting her go. She deserved to be wooed, he knew that. This holiday, he decided that he would show her what being married to him would be like, and what making a family with him meant for their future. Jax would marry Cassidy, of that he was sure, he just wanted to make sure that she knew how he felt about her before he asked her, he didn't want her to think that he was only asking for their babies' sake.

CHAPTER TWENTY-TWO - CASSIDY

Cassidy woke up and rolled over, stretching her arms high above her head with a satisfied sigh. She and Jax had been in Bingara for a week now, and things couldn't be more perfect. While no one commented on it, Cassidy knew from the smiles they kept giving her and Jax, that his family knew things had shifted between them. Cassidy was glad that they knew, there was no way that she could have refrained from touching Jax now that the two of them had started a physical relationship, every second she was with him her skin craved his touch, and her fingers itched to be stroking him, her very being buzzed with the need to be closer to him. No, she definitely could not have hidden that, her longing. Cassidy was starting to realise that her feelings ran deeper than that, that maybe she had fallen in love with Jax somewhere along the way, but she hadn't voiced her thoughts to Jax, not wanting to scare him lest he didn't feel that same way, or worse, if it was just her hormones playing up.

Jax had already left the bed, his side cold, empty except for a note, reminding her that they were hosting a barbecue today and that she should take her time and relax, he would be outside setting everything up if she needed him. Cassidy happily took his advice, lingering in the hot shower for longer than she normally would have. Jax had been spoiling her rotten this week, and she relished it. he had made her feel spoilt and wanted and had refused to let her do anything, exclaiming that growing two babies was work enough for her. Cassidy wasn't sure how she had gotten so lucky. Once she had finished dressing in a knee-length blue shift dress, one of Jax's favourites, she slipped into matching sandals and pulled her hair into a ponytail, before wandering outside to find Jax.

"Hello beautiful," he whispered from behind, sliding his arm around her waist and resting his chin on her shoulder, his hand splayed out across her stomach, feeling the babies twist and move inside her. "Did you sleep well?"

"Mm-hmm," Cassidy answered, "do you need any help?" She twisted in Jax's arms to look up into his face.

"Not a chance," Kyle called from the other side of the yard, "I remember when Jules was six months pregnant, and she wasn't having twins. No, you just go sit over there," Kyle pointed to a table in the shade, where Judy and Jules were busy untangling fairy lights, "and look after those nephews of mine."

"Honestly," Cassidy muttered, "anyone would think that I was made of glass. Jax?" She looked at him questioningly.

"Nope, I'm siding with Kyle on this," he said, kissing her quickly.

"Fine," Cassidy spoke, "I'll go and sit down, but only because I know how much you both care about these babies." She sat down carefully, the truth was, she was glad to be sitting, she was tired all the time now, and she still had three more months to go. She helped Judy and Jules to untangle the lights, and then kept an eye on Amy and Max while they went to string the lights up throughout the yard. Cassidy thought it odd that they were stringing fairy lights for a daytime barbecue, but when she mentioned it she discovered that Judy adored fairy lights, and according to her, it wasn't a party without them.

Judy really had gone all out for the barbecue, for no particular reason, just an excuse to catch up with all the family while Jax was at home.

189

Cassidy thought that it was very sweet that so many people had come, she must have met all of his relatives by now, she was sure of it. The trestle tables were laden down with food, Cassidy laughing to herself to see that Judy had included a couple of dishes that she had labelled For Cassidy Only, as if anyone else would want to eat her cinnamon doughnuts covered in gherkins! Excusing herself from a conversation with Jax's aunt, Cassidy waddled across the lawn, heading for the barbecue and Jax, who was manning it with most of his male cousins. Obviously a male thing, Cassidy smiled to herself. As she watched Jax's face, his expression changed from easy and casual to scowling, and she glanced behind her to see what had irked him, seeing Tara striding in on the arm of a man Cassidy was yet to meet.

"Jax?" As she reached his side she wrapped her arms around his waist, looking up into his face. "Are you okay?"

"Everything's fine," he assured her with a smile, "I'm going to grab more ice."

"He's lucky to have you, Cassidy," the compliment came from one of Jax's many cousins.

"Thank you," Cassidy replied.

"I can't believe you two are having twins, that's so wild!" Another cousin joined the conversation. "Do you guys have names chosen yet?"

"No," Cassidy smiled, "we decided not to find out the genders of the twins, we want to be surprised, although I think they are girls," Cassidy spoke with Jax's cousins about name ideas for a while longer, all of them keen to share their suggestions for names, ranging from Charlotte and Thomas, which Cassidy loved, to the more unusual Lyric and Tempo, which Cassidy was too polite to comment on. It was a good ten minutes since Jax had left, and Cassidy was starting to wonder where he had gotten to. She excused herself and waddled towards the house, her eyes scanning the backyard and not locating Jax. Cassidy walked inside, looking for Jax. Seriously, how long does it take to get more ice? She smiled indulgently, knowing Jax, he had most likely become distracted by his new song and was sitting somewhere, scribbling down lyrics.

"Jax?" She called, walking into the kitchen, and looking around. "What the heck?!" There, right in front of her, was Tara, kissing Jax. Seeing red, Cassidy marched across the room

191

and grabbed Tara's arm, physically ripping her off Jax with a growl. "What a nasty little habit you have, Tara, trying to steal things that don't belong to you."

"It's hardly stealing when he wants to come," Tara smirked.

"Delusional too I see," Cassidy tut-tutted, "what a pity."

"You see Tara, while you might be pining after Jax and hoping that he comes back to you, he's moved on." Cassidy crossed her arms over her ample chest and smirked at Tara. "He's settled down, made a commitment, he's becoming a father. He doesn't need you, in fact, he hasn't even thought about you in months, Tara. So, while you might need him, he sure as heck doesn't need you. I suggest you leave, and when I say suggest, I mean go now or I'll have Tony and Kane escort you out," Cassidy hissed at the other woman, not breaking eye contact or backing down until she saw her slink outside, only then did Cassidy move, following her to make sure she left the barbecue.

CHAPTER TWENTY-THREE - JAX

Annoyed with himself, and livid with Tara, Jax storms outside and past the barbecue and his waiting cousins, who share a look amongst themselves before all following him as a group, gesturing for Tony to take over the manning of the barbecue. Jax didn't stop until he was in the garage, guitar in his hand, angrily strumming away.

"Jax, what happened?" Kyle was the one who broke the silence.

"Tara," he bit out.

"What do you mean, Tara?" Kyle looked worried. "Please tell me you didn't do anything stupid."

"Of course not," Jax said sarcastically, "unless you count kissing Tara in the kitchen and being walked in on by Cassidy, stupid, in which case, yes, I did."

"Jax, what the heck?!"

"I stuffed it all up, okay, are you happy now? I ruined it all, just like I always do. Cassidy is probably inside right now, packing her bags to go back to Alice Springs, I doubt I'll ever see her again, heck, I'll be lucky if she lets me see the twins," Jax raved, loathing and self-pity flowing fast, threatening to drown him.

"Jax," Kyle stepped forward, "that's not what I meant. What happened?"

"I don't," Jax shook his head, "I mean," he sighed, "I don't want to drag you into my mess."

"Don't be ridiculous," his cousin spoke with a mischievous glint in his eye, "we're your friends, and your cousins, our entire job is to lead each other into trouble and help each other get out of it." He sat on the lounge and propped his feet up on the makeshift coffee table they concocted years earlier from some found milk crates. "Now, spill." All of Jax's other cousins followed suit, sitting wherever they could fit, looking at him, waiting for him to explain, not judgement in their gazes, only concern and love.

"Tara followed me into the kitchen while Cassidy was with you, tried to convince me to give us another go, as if I ever would, that ship sailed a long time ago, even before she caused mum such pain. When I told her that I had moved on, that I was happy now, she thought she could convince me otherwise."

"By kissing you?" Kyle clarified.

"Yes," Jax nodded.

"Well, there you go then," Kyle crowed, triumphantly, "it wasn't you kissing her, it was her kissing you, I'm sure if you explain that to Cassidy, she'll understand."

"Would you?" Jax asked. "If you were six months pregnant and your partner had a history of being a jerk?"

"Jax, you're not a jerk, you just hadn't found the right person before now. Now that you have, you have changed, anyone can see that," Kyle explained gently.

"I just always screw up, what if that happens now? Cassidy needs me, the twins need me, what if I can't be what they need? What if I stuff it all up? I'd never forgive myself if I let that happen."

"So don't let it happen," Kyle stated simply.

"It isn't that easy," Jax sighed.

"Yes, it is," Kyle insisted, "it's exactly that easy. You do whatever it takes to keep your family together if that's what you want, you make the sacrifices, you make the choices, and if, in the end, it still isn't enough, at least you know that you did all that you could."

Jax knew his brother was right, he had never considered it before, but maybe it was that easy. After all, he knew that he loved Cassidy, not that he had told her yet, and he was intending to marry her, if she would have him, there was nothing that Jax wouldn't do to keep Cassidy and the babies safe, he knew that. It seemed that Kyle was right, Jax had chosen to do those things, it had been a choice he had made, willingly. He needed time to process everything before he went and apologised to Cassidy, before he asked her to forgive him. Outside the barbecue went on, if anyone noticed all of the cousins had disappeared, no one came searching for them, which Jax was grateful for. He heard Tony calling that the steaks were cooked, and sent his cousins on ahead, assuring them that he would be out soon and to save him a steak. Once they had left, Jax picked up his guitar and started strumming, the song he had started during his first visit home with Cassidy now fleshed out. "I don't want to hear about the silence, I heard it once or twice, in another life, gravity keep me grounded, keep me upside down, like love unbound, but if you need to take some time, to fight those demons in your mind, well, I don't mind, I'll use the time, because I love you, I love you, I love you, I hate you," he sang as the world melted away around him.

CHAPTER TWENTY-FOUR - CASSIDY

Cassidy waited until she saw the group of cousins leaving the garage before she strolled over there, winking at Kyle on her way past, to show him that she wasn't angry. She paused in the doorway, listening to Jax sing. She loved his voice, all scratchy and breathy, pure sin. She could listen to him singing all day and never tire of it.

"I don't want to hear about the silence, I heard it once or twice, in another life, gravity keep me grounded, keep me upside down, like love unbound, but if you need to take some time, to fight those demons in your mind, well, I don't mind, I'll use the time, because I love you, I love you, I love you, I hate you," he sang, unaware that he was being watched. She walked into the garage, loudly so as not to scare him, and stopped behind him, sliding her arms around his waist and hugging him tightly.

"Jax," she crooned, "are you okay?" Jax shifted slightly, leaning forward to place his guitar down on the couch, and turning around to face Cassidy.

"How can you stand there and ask me that?" Jax cupped her face gently. "After everything that's happened?"

"I can stand here and ask you that because I know you are hurting right now, blaming yourself, when you did nothing wrong."

"Cass-"

"No, Jax, you listen to me. I saw her kiss you, do you hear me? I saw her kiss you, not the other way around. She followed you, not the other way around. I meant what I said in the kitchen, you've moved on, you show me every day that you've moved on, that the twins and I are your priority now. If she can't see that, well, it's her problem, isn't it?" Cassidy shrugged, determined that she wasn't going to lose her future over some silly woman's misplaced idealisation and crush on Jax. "You see, Jax, the truth is, I love you, I am in love with you. I don't know when it happened or how it happened, but there you go, I love you, and I will do whatever it takes to protect the things I love. I'm sorry I didn't tell you earlier, I was scared of how you would react, worried that you might run out of fear, or even worse, that you might not feel that same way," Cassidy

199

confessed. There, it was out. If Jax didn't feel the same way so be it.

"Cassidy, are you serious right now?" Jax asked her.

"Yes," she said simply, before rushing to add, "but please don't feel that you have to say it back to me or that I expect it to be reciprocated, I just want you to know, no matter what happens-" Jax cut her off by claiming her mouth with his, his tongue clashing with hers, both fighting for dominance. The kiss was by no means gentle, rather it was full of lust and raw need, an insatiable hunger. It was Cassidy who broke the kiss, dazed, her fingers moving to touch her swollen lips, looking up at Jax.

"Cassidy, I love you, I am in love with you. I don't know when it happened or how it happened, but there you go, I love you," he echoed her own words back at her, grinning. "I didn't want to tell you either, I was scared you wouldn't feel the same way, I didn't want to risk being hurt by you, or being unable to be with you anymore, or being cut out of the twins' lives," he looked sheepish as he confessed to her. "I should have been honest before now; can you forgive me?"

"Jax, seriously? Of course, I do, if you'll forgive me?"

"I will," he answered before claiming her mouth again, this time with a kiss so slow and sensuous that it left Cassidy in absolutely no doubt of Jax's feelings for her.

"Cassidy?" He murmured in his ear as he started kissing down her neck.

"Hmm?" She sighed, utterly content.

"Marry me?" He whispered.

"Jax!" Cassidy's eyes flew open, and she found herself staring into Jax's perfect blue orbs, alight with love for her.

"Marry me and make me the happiest man alive?"

"Yes, yes, yes!" She squealed, launching herself into his arms, catching him unawares, both of them falling down onto the couch, laughing. "Jax," Cassidy smirked at him, "I think we should both go and eat."

"Trust the pregnant woman to be hungry," he teased.

"Actually," she scoffed, "I was thinking of you, you're going to need all of your energy tonight, pregnancy has other added benefits you know, besides constant hunger," she winked at him as she stood up and waddled out the garage door, squealing as Jax caught up to her and scooped her into his arms, kissing her thoroughly, not caring who saw them.

CHAPTER TWENTY-FIVE - JAX

Jax fiddled with his jacket nervously, shaking the fabric and rolling his shoulders.

"Leave it," his mother instructed, "you look perfect, Cassidy doesn't care what you are wearing anyway, you know that."

"Thanks, Mum, you're right." The one thing Jax had discovered about Cassidy when it had come to planning their wedding was that she really didn't care about any of the trimmings, she was far more interested in what their marriage would look like than in what their wedding day looked like. Just one more thing that he loved about her. They had set the date for exactly one month after he had proposed, not wanting to risk her travelling any later. They had invited their closest friends and family and had decided to get married in his parent's backyard, which had been transformed into a mecca of fairy lights and carnations, Cassidy's favourite flower. Kyle stood beside him, a lot more patient than Jax was, waiting for the last of their guests to find their seats before Cassidy would come out. Jax wished they would hurry up, he hadn't seen Cassidy at all today, having spent the night apart last night, and it had made him irritated, much to the amusement of his family.

Finally, the guests were seated and Kyle handed Jax his guitar, Jax having decided early on that he wanted to be the one to play Cassidy down the aisle. As he saw her round the corner of the house, resplendent in her soft, whimsical wedding gown, Jax started to tear up. Even seven months pregnant, she was stunning. She faltered slightly as she realised it was him playing, a huge, beaming smile appearing on her face as his love was reflected back at him. When she reached his side, he couldn't resist kissing her, holding his index finger up to the guests to signal that they just had to wait a moment, a chorus of chuckles reaching his ears. Satisfied, he turned to their celebrant and nodded, the ceremony starting to join him and Cassidy together for the rest of their mortal lives. Once they had exchanged the rings and signed their marriage certificate, they were declared husband and wife and he didn't hesitate to crush her to him in a searing kiss, their guests cheering.

They danced the night away under a million twinkling lights and feasted on a meal of roast beef with all of the trimmings, and a cake that his sister-in-law had baked at Cassidy's request, a multi-tier chocolate mud cake and orange cake creation that suited both of their tastes. It was a perfect evening full of love and family, of commitment and promise. Jax knew that in years to come he would look back on this day and remember just how utterly perfect it had been for them both.

CHAPTER TWENTY-SIX - CASSIDY

"Jax?" Cassidy looked down at the sleeping form of her husband, love etched across her face. He really was the most incredible man she had ever met. "Jax?" She prodded his side, hissing as another contraction ripped across her abdomen.

"Hmm? Come back to bed," even in his sleepy state he reached for her, to hold her close.

"Jax!" Cassidy all but yelled, irritation winning out.

"Cassidy?" Jax sat up, looking around. "What's wrong?"

"We need to go to the hospital, now," she moaned, rubbing her back. Urgh, the pain was so bad.

"What?!" Jax flew out of bed, flipping on the overhead light and throwing on the clothes he had pre-prepared and waiting on the armchair for the past week and a half now. "Okay, don't panic, everything's under control, everything's fine," he repeated over and over as he laced up his shoes.

"I wasn't panicking," Cassidy informed him with a huff.

"What? Oh, no, sweetheart, I was talking to myself," Jax looked sheepish as he came to stand with Cassidy, rubbing her back as another contraction hit.

Once it had subsided, Jax helped Cassidy to change, and grabbing her suitcase, led her out to the car. The ride to the hospital was quiet, both of them enjoying the last few moments with just the two of them before they became a family of four. Once they arrived at the hospital, the staff ushered them through to maternity and into a bed. It was still early stages of labour, but with Cassidy expecting twins, the staff weren't taking any risks. Once Cassidy was settled, Jax joined her on the bed and they rang his parents, who had travelled up the week before, to be on hand once the twins were born.

"Hello?" His mother's voice was groggy with sleep.

"Judy, it's Cass."

"Cass? Are you okay dear?"

"Hmm mm, mostly," Cassidy winked at Jax, "the contractions aren't that bad just yet."

"Oh, that's good to know dear, wait. What?!" There was a shuffling noise before Judy continued speaking. "Tony, get up, quick! We need to go, now! Cassidy's at the hospital, the twins are coming, oh, do hurry up Tony. We're on our way," she ended the call.

Judy and Tony arrived a short time later in a whirlwind of activity, Judy placing several bags down on the visitor's chair and rushing to Cassidy's side to wipe her forehead as she rode out another contraction, Jax holding her hand and her gaze, helping her to breathe through it. Once Cassidy's contraction had ended, she embraced her mother-in-law happily.

"I brought you a few things, dear, I wasn't sure what you might need, just some socks and slippers, snacks, books, well, whatever I could fit in really," Judy chuckled. The four of them passed the time quietly chatting, as per Cassidy's wishes, the room was kept as quiet as possible, with minimal disruptions. She had a very clear birth plan in place, and they were committed to helping her achieve it.

"Okay Cassidy, you have done so well sweetie, now it's time for you to push, okay?" The midwife whispered up to Cassidy, who nodded in response

"We'll be right outside, sweetheart," Judy leant down to kiss Cassidy's forehead, "this is a special time for you and Jax, the start of your future. Tony and I will wait for him to bring us the news."

With her parents-in-law out of the room, Cassidy was helped into a more comfortable position for her to deliver in, and two teams of doctors quietly entered the room. Although Cassidy's birth plan was very specific, she wanted no medical intervention unless necessary, her priority was keeping the babies safe.

"Okay, Cassidy," her midwife spoke again, "on this next contraction I want you to push as hard as you can all the way up to the count of ten, okay?" Cassidy looked at Jax and smiled.

"Are you ready?" She asked him.

"With you? Always," he bent and kissed her softly. Cassidy broke the kiss sooner than she wanted, not wanting to be distracted from the job she had yet to do. With his hand on her stomach, Cassidy knew that Jax could feel when her contractions started, and he began to count for her. "One, two, three, four, five, six, seven, eight, nine, ten."

"Good, Cassidy, we have a head," the midwife encouraged, "would you like to touch it?" At her nod, Jax helped Cassidy reach down between her legs to cradle their baby's head, and she watched as the look of awe spread across his face.

Cassidy was lost then in a fog of contractions and pushing, she could hear Jax whispering softly, encouraging her, but as far as she knew, they could have been alone in the room, everything else faded away until she heard the shrill cry of a newborn, her eyes fluttering open in wonder.

"Congratulations, Cassidy," the midwife said, smiling up at her. As per her birth plan, she wanted Jax to tell her the baby's gender, and she looked at him expectantly.

"Cass, we have a daughter!" He cried with joy as tears rolled down his face. "A girl, we have a daughter, and she is perfect." The midwife passed the baby to Jax, who brought her straight to Cassidy.

"Hello, precious one, mummy and daddy have waited so long for you," Cassidy kissed their daughter's head, "you are loved, and you are wanted, so very much." She winced as another contraction hit.

"Okay Cassidy, once more and then you can meet baby number two," the midwife urged, as Cassidy bore down again, bringing baby number two into the world and earning an angry cry in return.

"A boy, Cass, I have a son, we have a son and a daughter," Jax exclaimed over the new baby as he handed him to Cassidy, who repeated the welcome that she had given their daughter.

Once the new parents had hugged the twins, the doctors stepped in to check them over, declaring them perfectly healthy and happily handing them back to Cassidy and Jax. Cassidy and Jax sat with the twins for a while, just the four of them, before Cassidy finally nudged Jax and told him to go and get his parents. Judy and Tony followed Jax into the room a few moments later, all smiles, at the sight of Cassidy cradling the twins in both her arms.

"Mum, Tony, you have a grandson and a granddaughter," he announced, beaming. After many congratulations and hugs all around, the conversation turned to the babies' names.

"We have decided on Carter Glen and Jasmine Iris," Cassidy smiled across at Jax, who was currently cradling Jasmine in his arms." Long after Judy and Tony had returned to their hotel, and Carter and Jasmine were sleeping, Jax still lingered at Cassidy's side, his fingers entwined with hers.

"I love you, Cassidy, thank you, for making my world whole."

"I love you too, Jax, thank you for being everything I ever needed."

THE END

About The Author

An international bestselling and award-winning author of sweet contemporary romance, Kathleen's novels showcase thought-provoking plots and strong emotions that have been likened to a Hallmark movie. Featuring feisty heroines and strong heroes, where everyone gets a happily ever after.

To discover more about Kathleen:
https://linktr.ee/KathleenRyder

Read More of Kathleen's Books

www.ingramcontent.com/pod-product-compliance
Lightning Source LLC
Chambersburg PA
CBHW070606120726
47909CB00007B/2462